MW01713226

BOOK ONE

Lavish MERCY

THE KUBAN LEGACY SERIES

BOOK ONE

Lavish MERCY

WILMA DERKSEN

WORDSMITH AMITY PUBLISHERS

Lavish MERCY

WILMA DERKSEN

Cover Design and Book Layout by PearCreative.ca

Wordsmith Amity Publishers
Winnipeg, Manitoba, Canada
WilmaDerksen.com

ISBN 978-1-7770080-7-9 (Print)

Dedication

Dedicated to the love of my life, my husband Cliff Derksen, and to ‘Anna’. Also dedicated to my two amazing children, Odia and Syras, who played an important role in making this book possible.

Chapter ONE

RUSSIA 1904

Anna dreamed of being free as she lazily watched a fly buzz her bedroom window again and again knocking itself dizzy with each charge. Why couldn't it just drop down to the windowsill and crawl out the crack she had left open for fresh air? No—it had to attempt the impossible—valiantly, painfully and noisily—bouncing against the invisible barrier again and again, not letting her rest.

She raised her book. She could end the fly's misery. She paused, and then gently guided it, still bouncing all the way until with one last bounce, it flew through the crack right out of the room. Smiling, she watched, as it flew crazily into freedom.

It had found its freedom—would she ever find hers?

Anna snuggled down under the covers for one last moment to relish the warmth of her quilt.

"Anna!" The voice was piercingly sharp. "Are you up?" It was her stepmother's voice—a voice so shrill it could penetrate the entire house.

A familiar dread filled her as she scrambled out of bed, slipped into her cotton dress and made her way down the stairs, her heart pounding, wondering what ugly chore awaited her. She was almost twenty-three; her stepmother had no business commanding her around like a child. Most of her friends were already married.

But before she reached the kitchen, she heard a scream coming from the backyard. It was Nadia's scream. Anna rushed out the side door.

Nadia was under the grape arbor in hysterics. "The nest!" she screamed. "The swallow's nest has been destroyed." Sobbing wildly, she held the broken nest in her hand.

Anna froze. "Hush, Nadia," she whispered hoarsely. "Widow Wieler will hear you. You mustn't bring attention to yourself." But Nadia was beyond reasoning.

The back door of the summer kitchen flew open and Widow Wieler emerged, brandishing a broom, flushed with anger. "Shush, you pitiful girl. Shush—before everyone hears you. Don't you know that everyone is listening—watching us? You must behave."

The broom became a powerful weapon as it began to beat on the girl. Anna froze in horror, as she watched the broom applied with such force.

Over and over again the thuds resounded through the yard. As the wooden handle tore at the frail cotton dress, exposing wounded flesh. Nadia began to scream with pain.

"You're hurting her," Anna pleaded, grabbing the woman's flailing arm. "Stop."

The woman had always stopped short of drawing blood, but today she seemed possessed. She swung at Anna, sending her sprawling.

"Don't you defy me, Anna." The broom was waving in the air threateningly. "I am teaching this Russian how to control herself."

Anna scrambled to her feet and stood between her stepmother and Nadia.

Nadia continued to howl Russian words neither of them could understand.

The broom hesitated in the air. Then slowly, with great reluctance the menacing broom was lowered. "This girl never stops with the howling." Widow Wieler said finally.

Nadia's howl turned to sobs and the sobs turned into whimpers and then to murmurs. Slowly even the murmurs stopped.

The yard was filled with a thick, sickly silence.

"Now Anna, you can take her into the barn. But hurry! You are needed to help with the breakfast dishes."

Anna knelt down and touched Nadia's trembling shoulders softly. Whispering soothing words of comfort, she helped Nadia to her feet, and then guided her to the two small rooms in the back of the barn that served as servants' quarters. "I'm so sorry, Nadia, so dreadfully sorry."

She helped Nadia onto the bed, a bag of straw in the corner, took some of the salve they used for the cows and other animals, and began to treat the open wounds.

"It was only a swallow's nest, Nadia."

"It wasn't just a swallow's nest." There were tears running down her cheeks. "Swallows bring good fortune when they come to nest in the eaves of your house, Anna. I really thought there was hope that things might return to the way they were—when we were happy…."

"And?" Anna asked, gently applying bandages fashioned quickly from clean rags they used for washing the udders of the cows.

"When a swallow's nest is destroyed," Nadia took a deep shaky breath, "it means misfortune, some evil, will visit the house."

"It's only a superstition, Nadia. It was only a cat—my cat—doing what cats do—hunting for their next meal."

Nadia shook her head. "For you it is a superstition; for us it is true. That is the difference." She leaned back against the straw-filled pillows. Her dark brown eyes stared out at Anna, wide with sorrow. "It was your cat that brought this on us."

For a long time, they looked at each other, sharing their thoughts without words. These last two years they had shared so much they didn't need words.

Anna remembered how Nadia had come to them as a ten-year-old child. Anna's mother had found Nadia, a tiny child almost beaten to pulp, rescued her and raised her as almost one of the family. When Nadia was of age, she started to help with the household chores. Those had been fun, love-filled days. They had worked hard but somehow it hadn't seemed so difficult.

Everything had changed when Anna's mother died. Up to that point, it hadn't mattered much that her own birthfather had died when Anna was quite young, because the Mayor of the Kuban villages, her stepfather, the well-known Abram Franz, had always been a good father—distant perhaps, but good. But shortly after her mother's death, the Mayor had remarried. The woman, who had come to be known as "Widow Wieler" had introduced them all to hell. A huge imposing woman, she had immediately established her own children, Maria, Jakob, and Lisa as the legitimate children, demoting Anna and her younger brother, Aaron, to the status of slaves. The servants were banished to the barn and demoted to something less than slaves. Most of the servants had left.

"Why don't you leave this house, Nadia?" Anna asked. "There are so many good people in our village who are looking for reliable help. I could recommend you. Widow Wieler's outbursts are becoming more violent. Who knows what she'll do next? You must leave."

Nadia grimaced as she tried to find a more comfortable position on the bed. "Why don't you leave, Anna? You suffer just as much as I do. She humiliates you whenever she can. Why don't you leave?"

The question caught Anna off guard. She had never considered it. Where would she go? The only escape from the house was to get married and her stepfather was guarding that gate, discouraging any suitors who dared to approach her. She couldn't find work in her own community; her stepparents would make sure of that. And to escape into the Russian world was something she would never consider—only the excommunicated members of the community left the safe confines of their community to enter the hostile outside world. Besides, she needed to watch and protect her younger brother, Aaron, who was not yet ready to leave or become independent. And she needed to honor the memory of her mother. Her mother had wanted her to marry a good Mennonite man, and become a contributing, godly member of this peaceful and prosperous community; for that she needed to remain part of the community.

"I can't leave, Nadia. I have no place to go. This is my only home." Anna could feel her throat constrict. "But you don't have to stay. You have places you can go to."

"You could come to our village," Nadia suggested. "I could find you a place to stay. I'm often tempted to go and help my Uncle Boris—he wasn't there for me as a child but has often invited me to stay with him now and help him. He's a little unstable because of the violence he has experienced in the war but mostly he's okay. He's very lonely now that his wife has died.... I would take him up on his offer but I don't want to leave you."

Anna realized that Nadia was serious. There was a deep longing in the girl's eyes that disturbed her. She had never realized the extent of loyalty Nadia had for her. Nadia was staying because of her—and her alone. If something happened to Nadia, it would be her fault. "I can't leave—but we must get you out."

Nadia shook her head and closed her eyes. "I'm not leaving you. Remember—your mother brought me home with her because you wanted a sister. *Schwesters*—remember?—You better go before she beats you too. She's in a foul mood this morning."

Anna stood up, pushing back her dark auburn hair. "Things will get better—they have to. You stay in bed today." She pasted a smile on her lips. "I'll come back later to check on you and sneak you something good to eat."

When Anna entered the summer kitchen, she found her stepfather sitting at the kitchen table. The tiny man with a long, graying elfin beard was eating porridge from a huge bowl, a plate mounded with buns beside him. Anna's stepmother, the woman she continued to call the "Widow Wieler," was standing at the stove pouring prips, a dull imitation of coffee, from the kettle into two cups.

Widow Wieler had a way with the old stove. In the kitchen, she reigned supreme. There were skillets of potatoes already browned. Pots of borscht simmered gently on the back burner. There were huge batches of zwieback already cooling on the counter, with at least several loaves of white bread baking in the oven. Pans of apple plautz, browned to perfection, were cooling on the table.

"You're late," her stepfather said.

Anna pulled an apron from the pantry hook and slid it over her head, tying the strings around her waist. Breakfast was out of the question; she was late with her chores.

“The others are out already on the fields,” he continued.

Anna poured hot water from another kettle into the sink, added a bit of soap, and began piling the dirty dishes into the water. She didn’t dare turn around to look at them. She could hear the chair scraping as Widow Wieler sat down beside her husband, sighing softly as she shifted her considerable weight off her feet.

Something was wrong. First of all, they had let her sleep in. She was rarely allowed to be late for breakfast. Ordinarily she would have woken up on her own but she had read too late last night and had fallen into a deep sleep, exhausted. Now they were here together in the kitchen, having a second cup of prips, and though obviously annoyed, were not meting out punishments for her. By this time her stepfather was usually at the co-op, buying or selling something, taking care of some official duty, or visiting the other residents of the village—always pushing everyone to do better, work harder, and pray—pray—pray.

The water was scalding hot. She felt herself trembling. She was sick with disgust at the beating and the humiliation of feeling so. Her stomach was empty. Her long hair, still unbraided, kept falling into her face. If only she had brought a ribbon of some sort with her. Her fingers were aching from the hot water. Yet she could not let them know this. She had to keep her back to them. All she could think of was Nadia being swatted like a fly in the yard.

Widow Wieler cleared her throat. “We are expecting visitors this weekend from St. Petersburg, Russian officials.”

Anna piled the clean dishes on the rack.

"One of them, a Mikhail Kamensky, has written us a letter," added her stepfather.

Never before had they discussed any impending visits. When guests came, the slave children, Anna and Aaron, were expected to fade into the background, surfacing only to serve the guests an abundance of tasty, fresh food.

"He asked if he could see you," continued her stepfather in a flat tone. "Do you know why this Mikhail Kamensky would like to talk with you?"

Anna shook her head continuing to wash the dishes.

"Here it is in the letter. Read it." Her stepfather held up a letter. Dutifully, she went to the table and sat down on the bench. It wasn't unusual for her stepfather to ask her to read and interpret letters that came in from St. Petersburg. His Russian was poor. It was only recently that they as a German-speaking community were being forced to teach Russian in school as part of the new Russification program. But to read something for clarification—this was a first.

Quickly she read the letter written in Russian Cyrillic aloud for them both. When it came to the part that referred to her, she read slowly.

I understand that you have a daughter Anna. I would like to have some time with her when I visit you.

She laid the letter down. Both of them were watching her closely. "He must be referring to someone else," she said. "I know nothing about this." Why did this man have to mention her name? She had enough to deal with.

"It is you," her stepfather said, taking the letter and folding it carefully into its original form and stuffing it back into the envelope. "I hope your uncle had nothing to do with this."

Anna wondered as well. Her Aunt Martha had left the village years ago in disgrace, shunned by the church—moved to St. Petersburg and married Viktor Kamensky the love of her life.

When her mother was still alive and Minister Cornelius Neufeld was the lead pastor, no one seemed to mention it, but after her mother's death, now that the *Aeltester* George Loepky was ruling the community with an iron fist, references to the disgraced aunt were surfacing regularly.

It was as if now they, Anna and her brother, the only living relatives left, were being held responsible for their aunt's disgrace. As if they were going to be like their aunt, allow themselves to be seduced by a Russian soldier—impregnated, and throw away their loyalty and their faith, leave the village to live with the Russians.

What no one talked about was how Martha had been rejected before she had done anything wrong. As her mother had explained, Martha was just too beautiful for the village. She had been endowed with thick curly, blonde hair, gorgeous blue eyes and a wineglass figure that aroused the envy of all the women and the desire of all the men. Plus, she was a little too intelligent and slightly rebellious. She was her "own person" in a village who preferred submission, plainness in their women and naïve compliance. Martha was none of this. Already feeling on the outside, she was vulnerable to the attention of the young Russian officer who liked to stay in their home. It was inevitable that they found comfort in each other's arms resulting in her becoming pregnant—the gravest sin of all. At first evidence of the pregnancy, both were banished from the community and went to live in St. Petersburg, married, and seemed to find unusual happiness together.

Her mother was the only one who refused to adhere to the rules of shunning imposed on everyone and had kept in touch with Martha. But she had remained very secretive about it all not wanting to involve her own children and incriminate them in the rules of shunning. Apparently, Martha's husband Viktor had become quite successful as a manager of one of the estates whose owner had been friends of the Tsars. It was rumored that the baby had died at childbirth and Martha had remained childless until her early death. Her uncle had remained a widower until his last year… at least that's what she had heard. How could her uncle have had anything to do with this request from a Mikhail Kamensky? Perhaps Viktor's brother or uncle.

"I don't need to see him," she said, hoping that would ease their suspicion.

"That goes without question," her stepfather said sharply. "We don't want any of our children, especially you of marriageable age, having anything to do with the Russians. But we're still not quite sure what we should do, whether we should send you to be with Gertrude's sister, or keep you busy in the fields."

"I can stay out of sight," Anna offered. "He won't see me." To stay with her step aunt would be even worse than working the fields, she thought to herself.

"Yet, if he demands to see you, we cannot afford to cross him…." her stepfather said, taking another sip of his prips.

She waited tensely for their verdict.

Finally, her stepmother placed both her hands on the table pronouncing, "We need Anna in the fields, Abe. She can sleep with Nadia in the barn. She'll be our servant as long as he stays. What is the matter with that?"

"And what should we tell him?" the Mayor asked.

"We don't need to say anything. There is usually enough business for these men to keep themselves occupied without interfering with our family. We will see to it that he remains busy."

"How many days is he staying?" Anna asked cautiously.

"Two—if not more." He paused. "But he is already on his way and will be here Friday so we have time."

Her stepfather stood up, took his hat from the hook beside the door and left, allowing the screen door to slam behind him. Widow Wieler followed him out.

Anna went back to her chore of washing the mounds of dishes. She couldn't believe her good fortune. She had just been given permission to become invisible for two days and become one of the servants, and to remain outdoors for as long as this Mikhail Kamensky stayed in their home. For her stepparents this was a kind of banishment. For her it meant freedom to plan something with Nadia. They could go visit

Nadia's uncle, General Boris Balakirev, to pick up a new supply of Russian literature, pick blueberries along the river bank, and watch the Gypsies dance around their campfires at night, swim in the lagoon—do all the things that she hadn't been able to do since the Widow Wieler had moved into the house.

Chapter TWO

Six versts away in the town of Nyevinnomissk, Mikhail Kamensky shifted on his wooden stool by the bar so he could have a better view of the room. A Georgian soldier with a wooden leg had emerged from the back of the tavern and limped from table to table looking for a sympathetic ear. The thud of his wooden leg was disconcerting.

"Now that I've lost my leg no one wants to hire me," he said loudly." I can still put in a good day's work. I can do anything any of you can," he repeated to each person in the room who would listen to him, often taking a sip from an unattended glass. Everyone tried to ignore him until they could stand it no longer. Then they shouted insults at him.

Mikhail recognized him—he had seen the train accident in St. Petersburg that had caused the loss of the limb. Useless man—they should have left him to die. He had become nothing but a burden to society.

The Georgian had stopped by a table of Cossacks and pleaded with them for some money. One of the Cossacks got up suddenly, pushing his chair against the man, sending him sprawling.

Then a thick-tongued voice coming from the Cossacks' corner rose out of the din, cursing. "Work isn't the problem," the Cossack said loudly, raising his glass of vodka. "Rubles aren't the problem. I have rubles." A hush fell over the room. "Stealing a horse, a real horse in these god-forsaken mountains is the real problem." He stopped in a moody silence. "The revolutionaries want a horse. A special horse, and I can't find anyone to get this horse for me."

The hint of unlimited rubles was causing a stir.

Mikhail turned back to nurse his drink. This was exactly why he was here in this bar—to listen to the locals talk. This is what this tavern was locally known for. Even in St. Petersburg, anyone coming to do official business here in Southern Russia for the Tsar always frequented these premises to acquaint himself with what was happening in this part of the country.

Mikhail glanced at the owner, Lev Slepkov, who was standing behind the bar with a fat smile pasted to his lips. He looked stupid, as if nothing could penetrate the big head of his; yet his eyes were watching the Georgian. No one, not even a despised cripple was allowed to be abused in his tavern. In any other place the man would have been beaten by now—and thrown outside unattended. Yet because of Slepkov's attentive presence, the man survived—now sitting in a corner nursing a complimentary beer.

Slepkov's massive size discouraged anyone from challenging his authority, allowing his tavern to become an unusual sanctuary where the partnership of good conversation and vodka flowed freely and harmoniously.

The other attraction of the tavern was Slepkov's wife—a bosomy, coal-black eyed woman with voluptuous waist-length hair to match. She had a voice that was well loved by the customers—a voice that "could soothe the demons of the most tortured soul."

Mikhail noticed the peasants at a nearby table bend their heads closer together. Even in their drunken stupor they recognized an opportunity for quick money.

"We've stolen horses," one of the peasants said loudly.

The Cossack shook his head. "This one is different—quite magnificent. The Germans have it under lock and key—with guards. We've tried planting someone on the inside to steal it. But each time…" The man looked miserable.

A wiry Tartar moved closer to the Cossacks. "Tell me about the horse and everything you know about the village. For a price my friends and I can bring it to you."

The Cossack eyed the Tartar with interest. The Tartars were known for their kinship with horses.

A Gypsy moved closer. "You will need poison for their dog. We have poison."

Slepkov filled Kamensky's drink. "Your stallion is safe," he said. "In our barns all the horses are safe."

Kamensky nodded. "Whose horse do they have in mind?"

"George Loepky's—from the Kuban villages—their lead minister. I heard that he just bought one the other week. Loepky has an expensive taste in horses—for a pastor." Slepkov wiped away the ring of liquid left by the glass. "But what brings you here all the way from St. Petersburg?"

"Business mostly."

"Business with who?" Slepkov asked setting down a fresh bowl of sunflower seeds.

"Kuban villages."

Slepkov nodded.

"Do they come here?" Kamensky asked helping himself to the seeds.

"The Kuban Germans? The Mennonites? Never. The odd one who might be out of sorts—being pushed out—then they might spend some time here. But no, they are the only ones in this area who don't frequent the place." Automatically picking up a broom he began to sweep away the sunflower shells.

"Secretive?"

Slepkov looked up. "No. I wouldn't say that. They are just a people who keep to themselves. Religious, hard working—and the humblest, proudest people I know," he smiled, sweeping the debris into a pile at the edge of the bar. "People around here don't like these German Mennonites much but I don't have a quarrel with them. In fact, they supply me with the best wine and the best vodka for the most reasonable price."

"Really? I thought they didn't indulge."

"No—at least not that anyone would know. But they still know how to grow the grapes and brew the wine. Odd people, but most of them respectable. Do you have a quarrel with them?" He swept the pile of dirt onto a battered dustpan.

Mikhail Kamensky lowered his eyes. It was too early to reveal all his cards to this man who knew everyone, everything, and never forgot a thing. But it probably wouldn't hurt to have Slepkov assume that he was another Okhrana secret police agent coming to check on the Germans. For years now the Mennonites had been ordered to participate in the nation-wide Russification program that forced all ethnic groups to teach Russian in their schools and to refrain from using their first language in the streets or in their churches. If Slepkov thought he was an agent, he wouldn't suspect that there was another reason for coming. He was really here to find—Anna—that is if there really was an "Anna", which might be more difficult than he had at first thought. From the Okhrana dossier on the Mennonite people, he had learned that the Mennonite women were protected and shielded from any outside contact. To break through these strong cultural barriers might be more of a challenge than he had anticipated. He would try, of course. At first he would use charm. And if that didn't work, there was always force. His orders were to do "whatever it takes."

The other reason he was on this trip was to check up on the late tax payment. The Mennonites had to pay a handsome sum for their pacifism ideals, their privilege to not participate in the army. This peace tax had become an excellent source of revenue for the Tsar especially now that the revolution was again rearing its ugly head. The Romanovs were concerned that some of their income sources were beginning to dry up. The Kuban villages were behind in their payments which was unusual for a Mennonite community. Their excuse was that the villages were experiencing hard times, but the suspicion was that there might be an inside embezzler. The last agent had fingered a "Loepky." Slepkov's news that Loepky had just purchased another prize horse was not a good sign. If it was embezzlement, Mikhail's orders were to be ruthless—something that suited him just fine. He had no love for these Mennonite people. Even as he thought about them, he could feel his blood begin to thicken, his fists clench and his lower jaw turn to steel. It would satisfy a deep need of his to avenge his father and mother and make these people pay.

Kamensky looked up, not remembering the question that had evoked the internal ruminations or how much time he spent caught up in his thoughts. All he knew was that Slepkov was watching him closely. Kamensky wondered uneasily if this man, who seemed to be so skilled in reading people could also read his thoughts. Had he answered the question with his silence?

But Slepkov didn't press further. The man collected the empty glasses and stacked them in the sink. He then returned in a few minutes with another bottle.

"Something must be brewing. There seems to be a lot of you coming from St. Petersburg," Slepkov observed.

Kamensky looked up in surprise. Realizing too late that this was just what Slepkov was probably looking for—a reaction. "Who else has been here?" Kamensky asked casually.

"A few Okhrana agents—which is quite normal except that these agents were from the secret police department. Oh yes—and Vladimir—was here with his brother.... You must know Vladimir—socialist I think."

"What did Vladimir want?" Kamensky kept his eyes down—noticing a black beetle scuttle along the boards at his feet—a gruesome life form that seemed to pause at the sight of his boots. Mercilessly Kamensky squashed the beetle with his heel, hearing a satisfying crunch and crack.

"They were pretty closed mouthed about what they were doing," Slepkov said. Kamensky had a sense that even if they were closed mouthed, this man knew more than they suspected, and wasn't about to tell.

"They asked a lot about the Germans," Slepkov offered, filling his glass again. This time Kamensky shoved it aside. He'd had enough to drink. The man was pumping him for information. He needed to remain clear headed.

His mind was racing. Vladimir here in Southern Russia? Wanting to know about the Mennonites? What if Vladimir knew? What if Yakov, Vladimir's father, had overheard his father's last wish?

Perhaps he didn't have as much time as he thought. He was hoping to do research here in the Nyevinnomissk, rest—and leave for the Kuban settlement in a few days.

Now he would leave for the village tomorrow, earlier than anticipated. Actually it might be good to appear early—an element of surprise never hurt—at least one day early.

Mikhail Kamensky picked up his hat.

Later—much later—that evening on the north end of the Kuban villages, a guard stopped and listened. He thought he heard the soft hoot of a night owl and the scraping of boots. As he listened, he heard nothing but the gentle whisper of the wind. He walked further and then turned back at the end of the road to retrace his steps.

He scanned both sides of the wide road. Nothing seemed amiss. Yet he sensed that there was something moving in the night undetected—something that eluded his hearing and seeing.

The Tartars could be like that. They were little men who moved as spirits. The guard sniffed the air. He paused, sniffed again. He couldn't be sure but thought he detected the faint smell of their unwashed bodies.

His skin prickled. If they were lurking in the shadows, he knew their target would be the magnificent Loepky stallion locked securely away in the barn surrounded by guard dogs. There had been several attempts over the last month to steal the horse, but none of them had been successful. He quickened his step. They wouldn't be staging another attempt on his watch. Not on his watch!

He hurried into Loepky's yard. There were no dogs. He stopped and listened. He heard nothing. With his heart in his throat, he made his way through the darkness to the furthest corner of the barn and there he stumbled over the carcass of a guard dog. He was too late! There was a gaping hole in the stone wall just big enough for two men—and the horse was gone.

"I heard nothing," he told his fellow guards as they pieced the events together with the meager evidence. They lit their lanterns and examined the stall closely. Apparently, the Tartars had done the impossible again. They had enticed a spirited stallion to crawl on its knees without a sound through a man-sized hole in the wall. The stones had been loosened and quickly removed them while they clucked softly to the horse inside. By the time they squeezed their short frames through the hole, the black horse knew their voices and they could work from the inside, expanding the hole.

The rest was impossible to imagine. Had the horse thieves thrown a sack over the horse's head, tied double sacks around his hoofs and then pinching his nose brought the horse to its knees and shoved him gently through the hole?

The guards looked at the size of the hole in the wall. It was unbelievable! Only the Tartars who lived with the animals and understood them completely could have done this.

The guards spent the next few hours going through the scenario and evidence over and over so they could understand the mystery of how this horse had disappeared. But they could find nothing more. Finally they had to accept the fact that they would probably never know.

Experience had taught all the people of the Mennonite villages that anyone who dared pursue the Russian Tartars into the rolling hills would not find the horse. And chances were that they would not come home themselves.

In the morning, the guards faced an even bigger task, to break the news to Reverend Loepky that his prize horse had been stolen.

It would not be easy. Loepky would not take this well.

Chapter THREE

Cornelius Neufeld gave up trying to avoid the puddles. It had rained all day, turning the main street of the Kuban villages into a muddy river. He could feel the cool water begin to seep into his leather boots. He had chosen the wrong footwear for this walk. He had been called to this evening church meeting unexpectedly and there had been no time to change into his boots.

Any other time he would have enjoyed the village's aura of tranquility as he passed the houses. With the candles glowing brightly in the windows, the village exuded a warm ambiance of peace and goodwill. It went well with their self-proclaimed mission in life—to be a people of peace.

In truth, their little village was embroiled in one conflict after another. If it wasn't a debate over dancing, it was drinking. If it wasn't that, then it was controversy about dress, or about smoking. Accusations were abundant. In their village, it was impossible not to be rather too proud or too humble.

In this village any transgression could be brought before the church and judged hastily—often without sufficient evidence, resulting in the excommunication of some innocent victim. These disenfranchised members when evicted were forced to go into the world—the Russian world—where they were often seen as Germans, rather than Mennonites, and therefore viewed with suspicion given the day's political climate.

The dampness was triggering the arthritis in his feet. He was already miserable about being called to an unexpected church council meeting so late at night and now to have to endure wet, cold feet during the meeting would not be pleasant. He had heard that Anna was on the evening's agenda. Why her? What was going on?

The church elders were already sitting around the round oak table when he opened the door of the church meeting room. The air was humid and stuffy with hints of cabbage. The room was dimly lit with an oil lamp that hung from the ceiling.

Aeltester, George Loepky, their lead minister, and by far the most imposing presence in the room with his thick white hair, was sitting with his hands folded in front of him. His eyes were capable of assuming a hypnotic gaze whenever he preached sermons on hell fire and damnation. It was with these eyes that he controlled the entire meeting. Even now they roamed the room. Everyone had heard that his horse had been stolen last night. They had also heard that he had not taken this calmly. There had been too many horses stolen of late, he said. They needed to have better security, more guards. One of the guards had been fired, and another was given notice The air in the room was tense simply because Loepky was unusually tense.

Next to him was Isaac Thiessen, the deacon. He was a short, mouse-like character whose main focus seemed to be hiding his bald spot with the few strands of hair remaining to him. He always sided with Loepky.

Joseph Schellenberg, the trustee, was picking at his fingernails nervously. Thin as a rod, his skeletal frame was accentuated by the over-sized black suit and white shirt that he wore constantly, even on the hottest day of summer.

Sitting at the far end of the table, Neufeld saw *Oberschulz*, Abram Franz, the Mayor of both villages, looking miserable and out of place.

In the shadows was Neufeld's nephew, Johann Baerg, who had just moved to the Kuban villages from the mother colonies. The young man, twenty-eight, lanky with dark shaggy hair and cool blue eyes had already shown himself to have an exceptional understanding of business. His latest endeavor, turning unusable threshers into functioning machines and then selling them for a sizable profit, had established his reputation as a wealthy businessman in the mother colonies.

However, after the death of his father, Johann had decided to visit the Kuban to purchase a farm. Neufeld wasn't quite sure why Johann had chosen to settle here in the Kuban villages, which was at least 300 versts from the mother colonies and a place not highly regarded by their Mennonite conference leaders.

Neufeld couldn't help but wonder if it was an escape of some sort—to leave behind the reputation of his well-known father, who had enjoyed a long productive ministry in the Molotschna area so that he could build his own life here in a remote village away from his father's shadow.

He also wondered if Claus Rempel, well known for his financial success and business acumen here in the Kuban villages had in some way influenced Johann during his last visit to the Molotschna area. He could see how the two men had much in common.

Plus, Rempel had two eligible daughters, Beth and Rina which is probably why he had invited Johann to spend Sundays with them. There were rumors that Johann had been quite taken with Beth—to her father's delight—and had started seeing her. Beth was lovely. It would be a good match.

Not that any of this mattered, he was just glad that Johann had come, delighted in fact. They needed young men with his potential here in these villages. Especially now....

Johann had left early in the morning to start his search for a new farm. It couldn't have been successful because Johann was scowling, staring at the floor. Or did he share his aversion to these kinds of meetings?

"Good to see you Neufeld—even if you are late," Loepky welcomed him.

Neufeld nodded, shook the hands around the table, and then took his place opposite the Mayor.

The meeting began with the usual formalities—Bible reading, a short reflection, and then prayers around the table, everyone taking part, uttering long pious prayers that seemed to become more pious and eloquent as they went around the circle.

Loepky cleared his throat at the end of the prayers, a signal to start the meeting. "Tonight, we have three agenda items. One is to invite and welcome Johann into our midst. Will you say a few words, Johann?"

Johann leaned forward. "I'm here to buy a farm. I would like to settle here in your community. I am currently staying with my Uncle Cornelius." He smiled broadly.

Everyone nodded. All knew that their village would be considered fortunate indeed to have attracted such a person. They were well aware of Johann's father, the esteemed David Baerg.

Loepky restated his welcome in many ways till Johann, a little embarrassed at the enthusiastic greeting, leaned back, his smile disappearing.

"The next agenda item will be presented by the Mayor, Abram Franz. He is worried about his children, Anna and Aaron."

Neufeld felt his stomach knot. He feared this was the real reason for the meeting. His feet throbbed.

Franz had a squeaky voice when he was tense. "My daughter Anna has taken to reading scandalous Russian literature. She is reading Tolstoy. I would like to see her reprimanded by the elders and possibly warned that her behavior could have her excommunicated." The words were said in a rush—obviously rehearsed.

Neufeld closed his eyes momentarily. This was unheard of. Never before in all his years on the church council had a father ever informed on his own children! It was the elders and deacons who prowled around the community looking for "sinners." Then it was the parents who made appointments with the church council to plead for mercy and grace for their children to be given time to grow up and mature.

Franz continued, "And there is her younger brother, Aaron. He had taken to drinking."

Neufeld sat stunned. Why would a man do this? Anna with her flamboyant hair, her quick wit, her grace, was hardly someone you would want to ostracize. And the young lad, Aaron—the one with the beautiful hands who could draw and play piano—was hardly worth their attention. These were Elizabeth's gifted children.

Word was out that there had been a few suitors in line to ask for Anna's hand; yet Franz had declined them. If Anna was such a problem why not let her marry? Why try to have her banned from the village? What would be her future if she were sent out alone into the Russian countryside?

And what was this about Russian literature? No one had ever raised these concerns when Anna's mother, Elizabeth, who had also read Tolstoy and other Russian writers. Why raise it now? Anna's wide interests certainly hadn't influenced her in any negative way. She had been part of his Sunday School class for years. In fact, he had often wondered if it was her interest in writers, her extensive reading, that gave her a remarkable understanding of the stories in the Bible. She had an interesting and refreshing way of looking at Jesus' parables and interpreting and adapting them into everyday life. If anything, she was one of the more conscientious of his students, always completing her lesson on time and praying when asked. She was just a lovely person to have around, always respectful, thoughtful, always inquiring after his sick wife. Bringing plautz.

Why would Franz—or why would his second wife, the Widow Wieler—want these children out of the village? Neufeld paused to reflect. Then he remembered. Widow Gertrude Wieler and Elizabeth, Anna's mother, had been rivals in school—Elizabeth, the promising child, and Wieler the less attractive. The rivalry had come full circle now. Gertrude now had the power to eliminate Elizabeth's children, and thus any reminder of her former rival. Neufeld was overcome with a wave of the depressing powerlessness that he always felt at these meetings.

Rarely was mercy shown once the request was made; once a name was presented to the council. Why did he continue to come to these meetings? He wondered. How could he continue to participate in such injustices?

"Russian literature?" asked Isaac Thiessen.

"Yes, she is acquiring books. We aren't sure from whom. They were found under her bed by my dear wife Gertrude."

Neufeld was disgusted. He wanted to ask—and what was Gertrude doing under the bed? Not dusting surely! The woman wasn't that industrious. She was snooping and looking for some mischief.

Neufeld also knew that Gertrude had found and burned Elizabeth's diaries soon after she had moved into the house. Since then, Anna was smiling less often, growing thinner, more withdrawn. She was beginning to look like a haunted version of her former self. And how could Franz stand by and let this happen to Elizabeth's children? It had been Elizabeth's charm, her wisdom, and her skill that had landed him the position of Mayor in the first place.

Yet Neufeld could say nothing as he listened to the others continue to question the Mayor regarding the children; some even offered accolades of admiration for turning in his children. Neufeld wanted to leave but he forced himself to remain seated. He needed to be here, to continue to watch Loepky. Since he had taken over the lead pastor position, the village had been experiencing more and more problems. No one felt safe anymore. Money was disappearing and Loepky was becoming increasingly demanding and controlling. When would the people see past his charisma and notice the ambition?

Neufeld glanced at Johann. The young man's lower lip was curled as he watched the proceedings with keen interest. How long would it take until Johann figured it out? Neufeld wondered.

"How old is this, Anna?" Johann asked.

"Twenty-three."

"And what are her prospects?"

There was a long silence. Prospects? Marriage? There had been suitors, and she certainly was pretty enough, but Franz was not letting that happen soon. Probably—because Gertrude did not want to organize a wedding—not for Elizabeth's daughter.

"No good prospects," Franz said confidently.

“I suggest you wait,” said Johann flatly. Everyone was astounded that a newcomer int their midst would take leadership on this issue. “Give Anna and Aaron a year, and then revisit the situation.”

“A year?” Franz was shocked and a little dismayed.

“Yes—a year—that’s what we do with the young people in the mother colonies. Recently we have been losing too many to other sects in our community. We have learned to value our young people rather than judge them.”

“And I,” said Neufeld raising his hand, “second that motion.”

Loepky raised his eyebrows, a sure sign that he was angry. This move was unprecedented. And Loepky wasn’t quite sure what to make of fit.

“Since our visitor has made the motion, and it has been seconded, and the suggestion is reasonable, we should take this into serious consideration,” he said smoothly. He took a moment to scan the room. “We can revisit this in six months as suggested. Are there any objections?”

No one dared to note the discrepancy in the amount of time given, no one raised his hand. There were timid nods of assent. They were expected to make their decisions through consensus.

It was obvious that Abram was not pleased. He would make them all pay for making him face the fury of Widow Wieler.

Loepky cleared his throat again. “The next item is that Mikhail Kamensky is visiting our village.”

At the sound of the name, Neufeld felt the blood drain from his face.

"Do we know the exact intent of his visit, Franz?" Loepky asked.

Franz shook his head, his face drawn. "It could be the Russification program in our schools—and of course—the taxes."

Schellenberg paled. "I wasn't expecting someone this soon. We are behind, the crops haven't been as good, the expenses are rising for everything—and the taxes are steep."

The room suddenly became even stuffier. They were not used to being unable to pay their bills.

Neufeld leaned forward. "Did you say Viktor or Mikhail Kamensky?"

"Mikhail," answered Franz. "Do you know anything we should know, Cornelius?"

Neufeld shook his head. There was something about the name that rang alarm bells. This had not been a good evening. His eyes were watering from the stale air in the room; he felt as if he would suffocate and his feet were throbbing with pain. He hoped the meeting would end soon.

Loepky bent his head in prayer—a blessing that lasted ten minutes. When he was finished, everyone bolted from the dreary room.

Chapter FOUR

It was a stolen moment. Anna grabbed a bowl of strawberries, a glass of cold water and headed for her room. Everyone was gone. Both the Widow Wieler and the Mayor had left for Nyevinnomissk early in the morning taking most of the family with them. Aaron, her brother, was out with the servants, and Nadia, in the fields weeding the strawberry patch.

She had earned this moment. Canning fifty jars of jam, in record time, she felt she now deserved at least two hours of uninterrupted reading before beginning the supper preparations. There was truly nothing else to do. In anticipation of Mikhail Kamensky's arrival tomorrow, the house had been prepared for his stay and even an evening's reception—if required. The formalities of any diplomatic visit especially of this nature sometimes demanded a gala of some kind—mind you this would be a Mennonite version of a backyard village party.

In her bedroom, Anna pulled back the curtain, and raised the window a bit to let in the fresh air. Then she leaned over and pulled a tiny box from the bottom drawer of her dresser. Inside the box was a button brooch that her mother had given her. It was exquisite—considered much too ostentatious for their plain clothes and plain ways by the community so she never dared wear it openly. But on days like this, delicious days when she found time to read, she pinned it on the inside of her collar. Wearing the pin made her feel whole again.

Then she gathered pillows and plumped them into a perfect hollow, a makeshift lounge, on her bed. Reaching under her bed she pulled out a book and sank back into the pillows, opening the book by Dostoevsky.

It was her mother who had introduced her to the written world of Russian literature. They had often read out loud to each other and then, after the reading, discussed what the story had meant to both of them. Those talks, often late at night, had been heavenly, transcendent, truly of another world. They would become so absorbed in their thoughts and words; the night would dissolve into morning before they realized it. The next day they would bemoan their tiredness, but never their talks. Those were always treasures to be remembered and relived as long as possible.

Anna opened the book again and began to read.

Suddenly he found himself with Sonia; she had come to him silently, and sat by his side. It was still very early, and the morning air was not yet softened by the sun. Her face still bore traces of illness, and was very pale and wan. She glanced up at him....

She could hear her mother's voice. "All literature is about the human struggle to find love and meaning. Great literature is a quest for truth. It is always about good and evil; therefore, it includes God."

When others had called her mother's interest in Russian literature heretical, she had never tried to defend herself. Only later she would smile. "We think religion is all about determining right and wrong. It isn't, Anna. We strive too much to live by right and wrong—when really, we should live fully and adventurously and then strive to apply and exercise lavish mercy when we fail."

Anna hadn't really understood her mother then and wasn't quite sure she understood her now. But her life's quest was to someday understand those words. All she knew now was that the understanding of those words could only be found in the Bible—and that she studied on Sunday—and in Russian novels—those she read whenever she could sneak away.

Then she lost herself in the pages. She loved the romance of the words. *She glanced up at him affably, and timidly extended her hand, as of old. She always offered her hand in a timid fashion, as if doubtful whether it would be taken. But now he seized it with rapture.*

Faintly, Anna heard the sound of a horse trotting into the yard. How dare anyone disrupt her well-earned quiet time. She had waited too long for this moment. Surely someone else would look after the visitor. Perhaps they would go away on their own.

...and rapidly looked up in her face. Not a word was spoken, and her eyes sought the ground. They were alone....

There was a resounding knock on the door. Anna sighed, straightened and waited.

There was another knock. Anna hid the book, smoothed her hair wondering if she should also hide the strawberries—food was not allowed in the bedrooms, but decided against it.

There was a third knock, louder than the one before. Anna slowly made her way down the stairs hoping they would go away. It was probably Gypsies wanting some cookies.

There was a fourth knock. Anna opened the door tentatively. There standing in the doorway was a man in full uniform, tall, powerfully built, sporting a Gorky moustache and an expression of extreme impatience and irritability. Behind him she glimpsed the sight of a beautiful black stallion.

"I am Mikhail Kamensky from St. Petersburg. Is this the Franz residence?" he said in broken German.

Anna nodded. This was the man who had inquired after her—and whom she was not supposed to meet!

Yet here he stood before her—a formidable man. And there was absolutely no one around. It would be hours before any member of the family returned. How was she to conduct an official welcome? Bow? Curtsy? Introduce herself? No!! She could not introduce herself. That much she was certain! If she did that, her stepmother would beat her to an inch of her life. As she stared at him, she was very aware of her faded cotton dress and her unkempt hair.

Finally, she found her voice. "Please come in. This is the Franz residence. I will go and find someone from the family and let them know that you have arrived. Please, come and rest in the cool of the house. I have just finished some strawberry jam that will taste delicious with fresh buns." Her mouth was dry.

Mikhail Kamensky followed her into the dark recesses of the house. The entire house smelled of strawberries. The coolness of the house was a pleasant surprise. He felt strangely comfortable and at home. It all seemed vaguely familiar. Was it because of the stories his father had told? Strange!

"Where would you like to rest and wait?" Anna asked. Her hands were sweaty and trembling. "In the parlor? In the kitchen? Underneath the grape arbor in the yard? Or in a private room? We have prepared a room for you. You could take a rest in it if you wish." For once Anna was grateful for her stepmother's thoroughness and need to have everything done well in advance.

"What would you choose?" he asked.

She looked at him. He was so much younger than she had expected, thirty if that. And he looked so much like Aaron with his shock of black, unruly hair—his hazel eyes. Any other time she might have enjoyed getting to know this man, but now all she could think of was this panic feeling that he might realize who she was. Her mind had slowed down to a ponderous pace. She couldn't think clearly. Even his voice and his questions were being processed as if she were underwater—drowning.

"I…," she had forgotten what she had asked—and what he had said. All she knew was that she needed to somehow distract this man, because if he found out she was Anna, and they talked, she could be beaten, even Aaron could be beaten.

"Which place would you choose if you had to wait?" he asked.

She would choose her own room but that was because she always had a supply of books and needed a hiding place when she read them. But if she didn't have to hide, she would read underneath the grape arbor. That was by far the most comfortable and most interesting place to sit. One could see Mount Elbrus on a clear day.

She led him to the grape arbor. "I would choose this place," she said watching his reaction.

He nodded. "I understand why. It is beautiful back here. Your yard is very neat. The view is lovely." There were chickens roaming free in the yard; yet the yard was clean. There were cats being chased by pet rabbits huge and dominant.

Kamensky sat down in an old padded rocking chair and leaned back. The chair was seductive in its comfort.

She watched. In short order he would fall asleep as everyone did who dared to sit in it.

"This is very comfortable. Where is the family? I'm sorry that I came a day early." Mikhail Kamensky explained, "It was hard to get word to you." Not that he had tried.

"Most of them have gone to Nyevinnomissk to shop for the day. But Aaron is here. I will get him. He is the son." She looked down. Technically she wasn't lying—but she knew that her entire act was an untruth. She had never done anything like this before. She had been taught to be truthful, transparent—her yes to be yes, her nay to be nay.

"Can I get you something while you wait? We have prips," she said. Ordinarily they would serve something cold, like blueberry juice, or hot coffee—never prips—to the Russian officials. But she had nothing else.

"Prips—would be good. And a fresh bun with that strawberry jam."

In the kitchen, her fingers were trembling violently; she could barely pour the prips. She should have offered tea. Russians preferred tea. She felt sick. He was just being kind. That's why he had asked for prips. He stepmother would berate her for all of this. She filled a plate with fresh buns, strawberry jam, plautz and even a few cookies.

Taking a deep breath, she returned to the grape arbor. The man had slouched back into the chair, resting—already dozing.

Anna bent over him to set the cup of hot prips on the table beside him, He opened his eyes. Startled, she spilt the hot liquid all over his hand.

"Oh—I'm so sorry," she gasped. "So dreadfully sorry. I'll get you a cloth."

She laid the plate down on the table and rushed back into the kitchen. "Towel," she said to herself. "Dry off the hand—and apply a little salve." With great trepidation she returned with her supplies.

"It was nothing," he said as he showed her his hand. "Not even a red blotch."

That was not good either, Anna thought. No burn meant that the prips wasn't even hot. Prips was always supposed to be served hot; otherwise, it tasted even more like dishwater.

Dying of mortification, she backed away. "I can get you something cold to drink."

"No," he said gently. "I'm comfortable but do find someone to look after my horse. That would be enough."

"Oh yes," she gasped again. "Your horse. I will look after it. How rude of me." It was an escape….

"Is there no one else? The horse can wait…," he began to say.

But she would hear none of it. She had been trained to deal with a horse. She escaped to the front of the house to find the horse still tethered to the front post. It was obvious the stallion had been ridden hard all day. He looked weary, docile and quite harmless—an animal that would appreciate one of their clean stalls.

"Come on old boy. Let's get you comfortable." She untethered him and started to walk toward the barn, pulling on the reins gently, expecting the horse to follow meekly. But he didn't. With one angry snort, the horse transformed from a tired, travel-weary, nondescript horse into a young, magnificent stallion of strength and mastery. He reared on to his hind legs, ripping the reins from her hands. A hoof on the upswing knocked her hard against the hitching fence ripping her dress and sending her sprawling onto the ground. The horse landing on his feet, tossed his head, his mane rippling; he glared at her, daring her to try to touch his reins again. Anna lay on the ground, stunned and immobile.

Mikhail, appeared at the door. "Mishka!" The horse immediately lowered his head, as if understanding, and trotted over to his master, docile and demure, unrecognizable from the angry, indignant horse of a moment ago.

Anna scrambled to her feet. Gingerly she felt the open wound on her shoulder. Already the pain was beginning to sear through her entire body.

With one hand on the horse, Mikhail watched her. "I do apologize. The horse can wait. Let's look after you." He said about to tie the horse to the hitching post again.

Anna shook her head. "No, I'm fine. We need to take your horse out of the sun. I'll show you the way."

Without daring to look back, she showed him to the barn that was attached to the house in Mennonite style. Kamensky followed her leading the horse into a stall covered with fresh straw. While he rubbed the horse down, she brought pails of water from the cistern.

"Sorry the horse turned on you," Kamensky said again. "He's rather high spirited."

Anna nodded numbly. Her shoulder was throbbing, but she could not let on.

"Oats?"

Kamensky shook his head. "Perhaps a little later?"

Anna nodded. "We always wait until they're more relaxed too. I think he has taken to this stall. I think he will be comfortable."

"I agree—he will like staying here. He has seen much worse. This is cool, with few flies."

The horse nuzzled his owner.

"I need to go get the family," Anna said suddenly—again feeling remiss. "It will take me a few minutes." What does one do with a Russian official as he waits? If only she knew the answer.

"And I'll go back to the arbor. I just might snooze while I wait."

She led the way back to the grape arbor.

But before he sat down, he turned to her. "Now let's have a look at you," he said taking her arm to hold her while he examined her shoulder. "That's not good." He said leading her to the table, he now took the salve she had brought for his hand and applied it to her shoulder.

"I'm so sorry," he said again, gently fingering the rip in her dress.

That's when he saw the pin on the underside of the collar. A Fabergé pin. Unmistakably! An odd place for a pin of such worth. Who was this servant girl?

Anna clutched at her dress. Why hadn't she been more careful? Surely, he must think her without any decency—and seeing the pin would only arouse suspicions as to her real status.

"I need to change," she said awkwardly. "And then I need to go and find someone from the family."

She ran from the room before he could say anything.

She ran back to her room. ripped off the old dress, flung on a new one, and ran out the back door heading for the field. She needed to find them quickly.

She found Aaron, her brother, resting under a tree, his eyes closed. The servants, who were hoeing the blueberries, had outdistanced him a long time ago. Any other time she would have chided him for shirking his duties, knowing that both of them would be punished for his tardiness, but today she had other things on her mind. “Oh Aaron, you must come. Mikhail Kamensky has come early and is asking for someone from the family.”

“So?” One eye opened and then closed again.

Aaron was nineteen—but seemed much younger. He had never taken to working the fields like the others. He had an artistic temperament. Give him a musical instrument and it would sing. Give him a pencil, and it would draw. In school, he outshone all the other students. But give him something practical and he would dissolve into a state of lethargy.

“You must come,” she tugged at him. “You need to represent the family>”

Then she realized that she had never told her brother about any of it—the letter, the visit, the need to keep her identity secret. And none of it would matter to him; he was past caring. He was mired in his own despondency, sick and tired of being treated as a second-class citizen in his own home. In fact, he did everything he could to antagonize his stepparents. Telling him about her plight, about Mikhail, would only give him another opportunity to aggravate everyone. She could not give him this opportunity.

“Go back to sleep,” she said to Aaron, turning to race across the field toward Nadia.

“Nadia!” she called. “Nadia, I need you.”

Nadia stopped hoeing.

"Nadia, I don't know what to do." And then in one gush she began to explain. "He's here. He's sitting under the grape arbor. And Nadia, I've lied. I haven't really lied. But I lied by not telling him who I really was." Her eyes wide, she was trembling like a leaf.

Nadia put her arm around Anna's waist. "Let's go sit in the shade and you can tell me everything."

They walked to the edge of the field and found a small grove of trees. There, sitting on the grass, Anna took a deep breath and retold the story, slowly, bit by bit.

"You've never lied before, have you Anna?" Nadia asked, picking up a leaf and chewing on the end of it.

Anna shook her head. "Never to my knowledge. My family doesn't lie."

"Well," Nadia smiled broadly, "I have. Actually, I'm quite good at it."

Anna stared at Nadia in amazement. She had never thought that she would ever hear anyone bragging about being a good liar, or that those words would somehow make her feel better.

"If you can't lie, why don't you go back and just tell him the truth? Tell him that you are Anna, that you are family."

Anna shook her head. "I can't! I'm not to reveal my identity. This man is looking for me, at least that's what Widow Wieler and the Mayor think, and I've been told not to talk to this man under any circumstances. And you know that the Widow is in a dreadful mood of late; any wrong move on my part, and she'll punish me—and everyone else." The wound on her shoulder was continuing to throb. "Besides the man saw the brooch I sometimes wear—noticed it—and I could see the questions form in his eyes. He will come looking for me—so I can't be around to remind him.... I feel I need to leave. Out of sight—out of mind."

Nadia smiled. "Let me understand this. You can't go back. And you obviously don't trust Aaron to have the diplomacy to deal with this, and you have no idea when the family will come back. Yet this person can't be antagonized either."

"Yes, that's it exactly. Can you help me? Can you...," Anna was thinking hard. "Can you go back and pretend that I've been delayed, that the family is delayed, and you are there to serve him? That would be so good."

"And what will you do?"

"I want to go away. Since I heard that this man was coming, I've had my heart set on going to your uncle's place to pick up more books. Now I have an opportunity of staying two days away from here."

"And you think the Widow would allow this?"

"What can she say when I am gone? When I come back, I'll describe this awkward moment, and say there was just no way that I could imagine myself staying here and remaining out of sight now and unnoticed for the next while. I felt I would have been forced to reveal my identity. She will have to believe that it truly was best for me to leave for a while. If you cover for me, she won't notice—perhaps."

"Actually, it does sound like a good idea." Nadia leaned back against the tree trunk. "Yes, I think this could be a very good idea."

"Are you sure?" Anna was uncomfortable with Nadia's new attitude. What did she have in mind?

"Don't worry about this at all. You go and have fun. I'll look after everything I know the background story; you've given me all the details. I can do this Anna." She touched Anna's arm, looking determined. Her eyes were dancing. "How often do I get to serve a Russian officer?"

Anna felt her spirits lift. Perhaps this was an innocent enough solution. Nadia, who had proven herself long ago to be a master of any social situation, was consenting to do this. What harm was there?

"There is enough time for you to get there before it gets dark," Nadia whispered. "You need to make up your mind now."

"But what will your uncle think, my coming unannounced and staying there for two days?"

Nadia smiled. "My Uncle Boris adores you. He thrives on unexpected company, especially someone who shares his love for Russian literature. He still misses your mother, you know. My uncle is the least of your worries."

Anna nodded. "I need to do a few things before I leave."

"And I need to go and look after our guest." There was a wonderful light of mischief in her eyes.

Sneaking back into her room Anna took out an old sweater, threw a few dresses into a bag, took the precious jeweled brooch off the torn dress and pinned it to the one she was wearing. Then stealthily, she crept down the stairs, into the kitchen where she packed a bag of sausage, fresh buns, plautz, and cheese.

Then Anna slipped through the barn, past Kamensky's stallion, and down the path to the field to say good-bye to Aaron. He was in the shade of a tree, still half asleep. She called out to him giving a brief explanation of her plans but when he did not respond she shrugged her shoulders and continued on her way.

Whe took the well-known path that would take her to the Kuban River and eventually to General Boris.

Her step was light. Even the thoughts of the elaborate deception receded into the background at the thought of spending time in that wonderful Russian library; the dream of being away for two days gave her all the strength and energy she needed.

Chapter FIVE

"Knocked on the head once too often." That's what her mother had said. Nadia looked at herself in the broken mirror in her servant bedroom. She knew she was attractive—long hair, dark eyes, and full lips. The new dress that Anna had given her a few days ago fit her form perfectly. She was feeling physically strong. It was remarkable how it took her only a few days to recover from a beating. No one would guess that there was something wrong with her head from her physical appearance.

But it was moments like this, when she was about to do something important, that the words of her mother kept running through her tattered brain. No one knew how right her mother was.

There was something wrong with her head. She had known it even as a child. She had first realized it when she had started school. What others found easy to understand—like letters on a page—to her were dark little squiggles that all looked the same.

It wasn't only the learning. When she had come to the Mayor's house as a badly bruised and battered ten-year-old, Anna's mother had thought the injury was only physical but it wasn't. The physical pain Nadia understood. It was the inside pain, the invisible pain that had been worse. There were these dark inky patches in different places in her mind—black voids where she knew she could not go. To try and cross these dark spaces or even venture too close would suck her into a bottomless, windy blackness that could absorb her for days.

It was only Anna who seemed to know that there were places in her brain that didn't function. Anna said it had something to do with a fear of being left alone, deserted, and isolated. Some of it was true because Nadia knew that if she felt she was being sucked into the blackness, all she had to do was find Anna. It seemed only Anna could help her recover from these bouts of black despair.

It never bothered her to be out hoeing or weeding in the fields, to join friends at a party, or work in the kitchen. She was always with someone. It was only when she was alone that she could feel the pain. The fact that Anna would be gone for two days left her feeling uneasy. She could feel the dark patches widen ever so slightly.

Nadia combed her hair slowly, forcing herself to remain calm. She had learned much through the beatings. One was that there were two kinds of people; those who didn't beat others and those who did. Of those who beat others, there were two kinds—those who enjoyed beating others, and those who didn't enjoy it but couldn't help themselves. Her mother hadn't been able to help herself. Her Uncle Boris, the one with all of the Russian literature, couldn't help himself. Her father couldn't help himself. Most of her family couldn't help themselves. It was what they knew; they were trapped into hurting each other because of their own pain and confusion.

Widow Wieler was one of those who enjoyed beating others. Mayor Franz was someone who was too timid to beat anyone himself, but enjoyed watching his wife beat the servants and Anna. That was the sickest kind.

There were no ugly patches of confusion when it came to understanding these beatings. The only thing she didn't understand was why did they pick on her? Why did everyone relish beating her more than others? Was it that she appeared to be so strong? Or was it that she appeared weak? Was it that she would scream out with pain and—howl until they stopped?

No one beat Anna—except the Widow. She had beaten Anna once—and Anna hadn't cried. Anna had stood in the middle of the yard, unbending, allowing Widow Wieler to whip her with a willow stick endlessly till her dress was ripped to shreds and her back dripped with blood. Anna had stood there, eyes closed, with regal dignity till Widow Wieler had exhausted herself. Then Anna had gone to her room and isolated herself, only allowing Nadia to come into the room. The entire time Nadia had nursed the wounds, Anna hadn't whimpered or complained. Once the bandages were off Anna had gone down to the river and washed the torn dress. She had pressed the dress, wrapped it in tissue paper and laid it in a box. Only as the dress was put away did Nadia detect tears. The box was placed on top of the wardrobe.

Widow Wieler continued to threaten to beat Anna but never had. The tension between them remained intolerable.

After that Nadia had decided that it was better to howl during the beatings. Even though she didn't like beatings—she had become used to them.

And this is where it became confusing….

Nadia tried to pin up her hair but it was too heavy; instead, she ran a comb through it and left it long. She smiled at her reflection. "Not bad." She smiled at herself again, pleased.

Playing host to this Mikhail Kamensky to protect Anna from her family was not confusing. She knew how to do this. She could even enjoy this.

Nadia poured out the stale prips and brewed a good cup of coffee, prepared a dinner of cold roast beef, potatoes, gravy and carrots. Then she retrieved a jar of blueberry juice from the cool cellar. When the perfect table was set, she went out to the grape arbor.

She stood silently beside the sleeping man in the rocking chair until her quiet presence aroused him. She waited patiently as his eyes focused on her. When he had regained his composure, she held out her hand.

"I welcome you, Mikhail Kamensky, to our home."

Mikhail stood up to shake her hand. He was confused. This girl who looked Russian had said "our home" as if she was family.

"I'm pleased to be here," he said automatically. "Has the entire family returned?"

"No—not yet," Nadia smiled. "Why don't you come to the parlor for your dinner and we can talk? The family will return later tonight. They always come home late when they go to Nyevinnomissk. I was staying with an aunt and was told you came early."

Nadia turned to lead the way through the house to the parlor. As she passed through the kitchen, she noticed a shadow moving just outside the window. Were the servants back from the fields? But usually, they didn't come to the kitchen. They stayed outside, eating from the summer kitchen and then spending their evenings either by the river or playing card games in the north yard behind the barn. She paused. There was something odd about that shadow.

She opened the screen door leading the way into the parlor where the table was set. "I hope this will be to your liking," she said, gesturing for him to seat himself comfortably on the sofa.

"Am I dining alone?" he asked, noticing the single table setting.

She nodded. "Unless you wish me to join you?"

He nodded. "Please."

She fetched a plate of food for herself and sat opposite him, relishing the opportunity to eat in the beautiful parlor where she had been forbidden to enter since Widow Wieler had moved into the house.

"Your name?"

Nadia paused. She needed to consider this carefully. What would be best? To conjure up an imaginary member of the family and pretend that there was an "Anna?" Or would it be better to be Anna and see what this was all about? She didn't want to think too long—she did want to surprise Widow Wieler.

"Anna," she said watching him closely for his reaction. "I am Elizabeth's daughter."

His eyes fastened on her immediately with new intensity. It was what she was hoping for. Anna's description of this man, and the family suspicions were correct. This man was looking for Anna. Yet she needed to remain unaffected by his attention.

"I was hoping to meet with you," he said. He appraised her again. Her beautiful olive skin shone with health and vitality. Her huge dark eyes, thick black hair and beautiful engaging smile were such a pleasant surprise. This personality was open, friendly; it wouldn't be hard to relate to her, even gain her trust, if he remained charming. The young woman with the auburn hair worn in braids this morning was more reserved—it would have been difficult dealing with her.

"Yes—my father mentioned that you wanted to meet me." Nadia smiled.

Mikhail began to eat with relish. "This roast beef is wonderful. Everything is good."

Nadia nodded. "Thank you." Her own food wasn't tasty. It was as if her mouth wasn't functioning at all.

He took a long drink of blueberry juice. "This has been perfect." He shoved his plate aside. "Actually, this will work out nicely to talk to you without your family here," he said half to himself, half to her. "Have you lived here all your life, Anna?"

Nadia was glad now that she had spent so much time with Anna. She knew Anna's personal story as if it were her own. "I moved to this house after my father died and my mother remarried the Mayor. The Mayor was very good to us."

"And your mother?"

"She died a few years ago. And the Mayor remarried a woman known as Widow Wieler."

Mikhail nodded. "Were you close to your mother?" He leaned forward.

"Oh, yes." This Nadia answered as herself and as Anna. She had felt very close to this magnificent woman named Elizabeth. It had been Elizabeth who had brought her here to live. At that time the servants had lived in the back rooms of the house and had been part of the family, eating with them, sharing evening and morning devotions with them. And often, when she wasn't too tired, she had spent time listening to Elizabeth and Anna talk into the wee hours of the morning. She had always felt included.

"Tell me about your mother." Mikhail tried not to show his enthusiasm or his deep interest in every word, every gesture she made. He had to remain cool… detached….

Nadia could feel the warmth of Elizabeth's presence as she began to describe her. "She was beautiful. She was kind…. She was generous…. When she talked, everyone listened. She could see things no one else could see. She knew things no one else knew. She made everyone feel special."

She went on and on. Mikhail would ask a question and she would supply the details—time flew.

Nadia allowed her eyes to drift. It was getting dark outside now. Any minute the family would be coming home. Again, she saw a movement by the window. Someone was outside the window! She jumped up and ran to the window. The shadow was rounding the corner.

She ran to the front door, opened it and heard the bushes rustle.

"Someone was listening," she said flatly, turning to Mikhail who was standing right behind her watching her. "Why would someone be listening to us?" she asked.

"How would I know? Perhaps it was a cat? A dog? You have so many animals running freely. It could be any of them."

"This was different," she said.

Returning to the parlor, she began to clear the dishes. "Would you like something else? Perhaps rhubarb crumble cake?" It was her favorite. She hoped he would say yes.

"No, I think I've had too much to eat already. I'm not used to eating such good food when I'm traveling. But when you are finished clearing the dishes, you could join me over another cup of coffee. And then we can continue."

Nadia nodded, but felt uneasy. Something was wrong. Even now, she could still hear strange noises in the yard. The night seemed alive with a strange restless presence.

She carried the dishes to the kitchen and began to put the food away, and wash the dirty plates. That's when she remembered that there were still glasses and plates—perhaps even food—under the grape arbor. Widow Wieler would be beside herself if she found anything left in the yard overnight. "It attracts animals, thieves," she always said.

Nadia wiped her hands on her apron and opened the screened backdoor. The evening was warm, scented with the lilac bush still in bloom….

She heard a scraping sound behind her. She whirled around, but it was too late. A large, cold hand clamped her mouth while another arm pinned her to a strange male body that smelled of hay, sweat and horses.

"Shhhh."

A cloth was placed on her nose. She couldn't breathe. She tried to struggle against the arms that imprisoned her—but slowly it all faded and she was falling into the windy darkness. She tried to scream—her only defense against the fear. But she couldn't scream. She couldn't think. She felt herself succumbing to the blackness—the horrible, horrible darkness.

Chapter SIX

After a time, when Nadia didn't return, Mikhail began to wonder. Something was wrong. He went to check the grape arbor, the front yard and then went back to the parlor.

He sat down and listened. The house was empty. Where was everyone? First of all, there was the absent family who had said they would be home. Then the first servant wearing that amazing Fabergé brooch, looking like a Mennonite but claiming to be a servant—a clumsy one at that. Then this Anna—who looked and acted Russian. Her German was poor, her Russian excellent. Even her mannerisms were Russian; yet she claimed to be a Mennonite.

He was spending more time alone in this house than he did in his own. Where did everyone disappear to? Why was this house so strange—and yet so familiar? The only thing that met with his expectations was the food—and the comfortable home. He should be enjoying this.

But he was becoming increasingly more irritated with the smugness, the orderliness, the arrogance of the house—and the empty piety. All the things his father had told him about this place were now staring him in the face. His father had at first loved this community, had loved serving here—visiting it and staying as a guest in these houses.

Unfortunately, when they had found out—they had banned him from ever coming again—even complaining to his superiors. His father hadn't said much—but it was the pain, the hurt, and the hollow longing in his voice whenever he did talk about the Kuban villages that Mikhail could still feel.

Just as he was about to get up, and check the house again, the parlor door flung open and a young man, rushed into the room—a large stick in his hand wielding it menacingly.

Mikhail was on his feet, whipping out a knife sheathed in his belt.

The young man stepped back, suddenly looking uncertain about what to do next. Poised with knife in hand, Mikhail had one second to study the man with the stick. Scared that's what he was, a scared young Mennonite man, with the homemade clothes, short hair, and trembling lip. He reeked of drink. "Slow. Take it slow," he told himself. This was probably one of the family.

He put down his knife. "I'm Mikhail Kamensky from St. Petersburg, expected houseguest. Who are you?" Mikhail said in a low, cautious voice—the kind of voice one uses to calm a scared animal.

Aaron put down the stick. "What are you doing here?"

"I am waiting for Abram Franz and his wife to return from Nyevinnomissk."

"Why don't I know about you—if you're a guest?"

Mikhail shook his head. Why hadn't this family member been told? "Anna was here a minute ago. Why don't you find her and ask her about me?"

"Anna?" Aaron could feel himself grow even tenser. Anna had stopped by on her way to Boris' estate to say goodbye hours ago. He had pretended to be sleeping but had noticed her none-the-less. "She was here? When?"

"Yes, she was here a few minutes ago. She just served me supper."

"I don't think so." Aaron stepped closer. "Did you see them?"

"Who?" Mikhail asked stepping back, putting his knife away.

"The ones who took Nadia?"

"Took Nadia? Who's Nadia?"

"Nadia was in the back, picking up the dishes minutes ago and three goons came grabbed her and took her away on their horses hidden in the bush out back. I was doing the chores. I...." Aaron paused. "Is that your horse in the barn?"

"Yes. I am an invited guest in your home."

Suddenly he was remembering. That's why the family had been so hyper and tense recently when there was talk about visitors. Aaron tried to think—Kamensky? "Who let you into this house?"

"A servant. She served me prips and then left to find a family member. Then Anna came in and served me supper. She just left to go…." Mikhail was about to say the backyard.

"What did Anna look like?"

"She had long, loose black hair, black eyes, good looking. Spoke wonderful Russian."

"That's Nadia. Anna has reddish auburn hair—braids."

"Are you sure?"

"Yes—Anna is my sister. I should know. Anna left for the country this afternoon."

"The servant who met me at the door, she had reddish hair, brown eyes. She wore a wonderful Fabergé brooch. I suspected…."

"That's Anna. She always wears that pin. Underneath something."

Mikhail nodded. "And who are you?"

"Anna's brother," Aaron ran a nervous hand through his thick hair. "I'm not sure what is going on. I saw three thugs grab Nadia, and make off on three horses but she wasn't screaming. Nadia is always screaming."

"Which direction?"

"Towards the Kuban River."

Mikhail studied the boy. He had been drinking. Was he telling the truth? None of it was making sense. The boy was agitated—best thing would be to distract him—send him on an errand—a mission. "We should look for her. Is there anyone who knows these parts—who could help?"

Aaron hesitated. "Jakob. He is strong. He is in charge of the servants. Nadia is his responsibility… He knows……."

"You got good horses?"

Aaron broke into a big smile. "The best."

Mikhail paused. The "goons" were probably Vladimir and his rebel friends. He could deal with that later—at the tavern. But for now, he needed to find Anna—before they discovered Nadia's true identity. He studied the agitated young man …. "Why don't the two of you go look—follow the trail. I'll stay here and wait for the family—and then I'll will join you later."

Nadia woke, her head throbbing, her stomach churning. She hadn't known it was possible to feel so intensely sick and still be able to breathe. She couldn't lift her head.

There was a light burning into her eyes, but when she tried to put her hand over the light, she discovered that she couldn't move; her wrists were tied behind her back.

"I think she's waking," a man said in a low, cautious tone.

Nadia tried to assess how many people were in the room. Every time she tried to move her head, oceans of darkness swept over her, making her feel nauseous. How was it possible to be so seasick without any water? She fought against it. But as she pushed ahead, she knew that she was drowning. There was no escaping; her hands and her feet were bound. She let the darkness overtake her again.

"Anna?" The voice was hovering over her. The breath reeked of whiskey, stale smoke, and dirty teeth.

She shook her head. "Not Anna."

"Are you going to deny you are Anna?"

"I'm not Anna!"

Powerful hands seized her shoulders and yanked her onto her feet, then let her drop back into the chair. A sharp, knife-like pain shot up her neck. She felt dizzy. When she tried to open her eyes, the edges remained dark. It was slowly dawning on her that this wasn't one of her old nightmares. This was reality. She was sitting on a chair, her hands tied behind her back, her feet pinned—and they, three men with unshaven faces, were trying to waken her. Then she remembered that someone had grabbed her under the grape arbor. They had taken her captive.

"Wake up, *bliatz*." One of the men smacked her across the face. The darkness was gone. All she saw was red—dark burning red.

She opened her eyes wide; she was now angry. She scanned the room—no windows, one candle, and rat-attracting garbage littered all over the floor.

She surveyed her captors. The men were obviously from St. Petersburg. She wasn't quite sure how she knew this; it probably had something to do with their clothes—their hats, their scarves were foreign. And even though they were unkempt, something about them suggested city life. White trash from the city, which was always worse. City rats were dirtier than country rats.

"You bastards, *loh*, filthy scum, low life. You good for nothing city rats!" she muttered under her breath. It felt better. "How dare you tie me up? You stupid, peasant vermin. You belly-crawling viper snakes. Go back to your caves where you belong. *Durak*!"

One of them hit her across the mouth. She let out an ear-splitting, blood-curdling screech.

She had lost her words. She couldn't think of anything worthy of these nasty swine and was emitting a high, eardrum-breaking scream. She screamed till her vocal cords ached.

With lightning speed, one of them backhanded her, knocking her off the chair. She hit the ground unexpectedly hard. She lay in the dirt for a time, her ears ringing, waiting for someone to kill her.

Instead, they pulled her onto the chair again. One of them grabbed her hair, forcing her to look into his face. He was even uglier close up. She spit in his face.

He hit her hard in the stomach. It was a long and desperate wait before she was able to draw in a breath of air again.

The silence was almost deafening. But she refused to give in. She stared at them defiantly.

The leader knelt down in front of her. "Where is it? You know what we're after. Just give it to us and we're gone."

Nadia was dumbfounded. "I have no idea…."

"We know you have it, Anna. Your mother gave it to you." This was not making sense. "I'm not Anna," she said, disgusted with the whole charade.

"You can't fool us. We heard you introduce yourself to Kamensky."

Nadia stared at them - so it was them underneath the parlor window.

He continued. "Kamensky is after it too. But it really belongs to us—the people of Russia."

"I'm not Anna. We fooled him."

"We?"

There was blood in her mouth. "Yes, Anna and I—fooled—Kamensky into thinking—I was Anna."

The leader looked over at the two others. "But why fool him if it wasn't to hide the Fabergé?"

"Fabergé?"

The leader peered at her closely.

"Why fool Kamensky if it wasn't to hide the jewels?"

Her mind was mud. How could she explain it to this man who continued to hurt her? The words weren't there. "Her parents—didn't want her to talk—to Kamensky." It was hard to get the words out.

"Who are you then?"

"Nadia." Her head throbbed.

He raised his eyebrows. "Do you know anything about the jewels?"

Nadia shook her head. "No." Her stomach was churning. Her neck felt as if it had hot rods piercing the back of her skull.

His eyes slit. "I don't believe you. If you're helping Anna, you most know something."

"No." Nadia was indignant.

"You might as well tell us—because we will get it out of you. We will force it out of you one way or another."

Nadia shook her head.

"You'll talk."

"No, I won't—I don't know."

He studied her for a long time. "But leaving you here to rot—in the dark—with the rats—no food, tied up—you'll talk."

In spite of herself, her eyes widened with fear.

He was fierce…. "Talk now—or we'll leave you here."

Nadia looked around the room. It could be a cellar at the bottom of a building or a shack—there was just no way of telling. It was an ugly place with garbage littering the floor—a place that rats loved to inhabit. She hated rats. She hated the darkness. How did he know?

"Comrades…. Let's leave her alone. One day should be long enough—by then she'll have no toes—no fingers."

Nadia drew in a quivering sob.

"Maybe we won't come back for a week. She'll be skin and bones—with no eyes, no ears. She'll be left with only a tongue to talk."

Nadia strained against the ropes. All of them began to pick up their bags, their guns. They moved to the door. They opened it slowly. It was dark outside.

"We aren't in any hurry for this information. We can go to the tavern and have us a good time for a few days."

They were almost out the door.

"Wait!" Nadia screamed.

The leader turned around.

"I can help you," Nadia said in a hoarse whisper. "Please don't leave me," she whimpered.

Chapter SEVEN

June was a lovely month in the Kuban. Anna took a deep, refreshing breath of the humid air. It was like a tonic. She could feel her muscles relaxing as she made her way down a winding, narrow path among beds of wild narcissi, buttercups and yarrow, their sweet fragrance swirling around her.

She was going to see her mother's good but unusual friend, a veteran, General Boris Balakirev of the Cossack army, who had fought in many of the Russian wars—too many.

Actually, her mother had met Vera, his wife, while she was browsing through a market in Nyevinnomissk. The fact that Elizabeth was a Mennonite woman looking at some Russian books for sale had caught Vera's eye. Since she spoke fluent German, Vera had approached her mother offering her help. They had talked and soon realized that they shared a common interest in Russian books—enough to cement a lifelong friendship.

Her mother often talked about the first time she had met Vera's husband, Boris, a short man of mixed Tartar and Russian blood. He had an exotic appearance that matched his unusual brick house built on an estate.

Later she had discovered that Boris, who was an illegitimate child, had inherited the estate from his father, an esteemed and wealthy Russian nobleman.

From Vera she learned that Boris had settled here with every intention of becoming a good farmer after the wars but he could never leave the army experience behind. He always wore his army uniform and carried many kinds of weapons, some concealed under his clothes and others not concealed at all.

From Vera, she had also learned that this obsession with guns had been manageable at first but as he was getting older the soldier persona was in control more often. Boris was becoming more and more a man of imaginary wars. Some in the community considered him dangerous—and sometimes he was—especially when the_full moon awakened all of his war imaginings. But more often than not, he was a struggling farmer like all the rest.

Her mother had been more interested in the side of him that most of his neighbors didn't know, and that was his love of Russian literature that he shared with his wife. During his years in St. Petersburg, he had been exposed to the intelligentsia and the arts community from whom he had acquired a huge library of dusty, old books. It was said that some of the writers, like Tolstoy, had met him, liked him and stayed with him. He denied it all.

Boris spelled liberty—not a particularly popular word among Mennonites—not nearly as valued as words like peace or faith, discipline, hard work, contentment, simplicity, and honesty.

"We're not quite like other people," her mother had been fond of saying. "We're different." And then she would tell the story of how during the Reformation in the 1500s, their leader Menno Simons followed Martin Luther's example in breaking away from the Catholic Church. But Menno Simons had been more radical in that he had abandoned infant baptism for adult baptism, and even more important, he had preached "peace"—a non-violent way of living. The story was told that during the ensuing persecutions, Simons' brother had fought back against his persecutors. One of his violent initiatives ended in an ugly massacre. It had been a moment of enlightenment for Menno Simons; seeing the result of violence, he had chosen "peace" and martyrdom for his followers.

"We would prefer to die than to kill," her mother would say proudly, "and for that we have never been appreciated in most of the countries we have lived. They would prefer that we would participate in their wars."

If her mother was proud of being Mennonite that day, she would elaborate on the courage of the martyrs. Sometimes, she was disgusted with the church. "We speak about peace and love, but all we do is fight with each other."

Then her mother would talk proudly of the invitation of Catherine the Great, as if it were personal, to come settle in her country. And how the first main settlement had been in the Ukraine, from where clusters of families had continued to emigrate, for various reasons, to different parts of Russia.

Anna reached a little hill overlooking the two villages where they lived.

Here her mother had always paused explaining how a group of Mennonites moved to Southern Russia to the Kuban Valley about forty years ago to begin two new communities, Alexandrodar, the lower village, separated by a ridge of hills, and Vyelikoknyazheskoye, the upper village, in the shadow of the Caucasus Mountain range.

"And that's why we are here, in this country of plenty that produces such sweet fruit, perfect grapes." Her mother loved to prepare food with fruit on top of everything.

Anna slowed down when the ground started rising and becoming rockier. She was nearing the river. The Kuban River was young, fresh from mountain springs hidden in the Caucasus. It had for years nibbled at its soft river banks, growing broader and spawning increasingly more tributaries. that cut through the well-known path, changing it constantly.

As she moved further and further from the village, she realized she had never walked alone in the country. It was forbidden for any of them to leave the village alone, even to pick blueberries or raspberries because of the roving bands of Tartars, Gypsies, and Cossacks always looking to either steal or create disturbances. There were countless stories of women being raped or threatened. There were also wolves and wild packs of abandoned Russian dogs. Yet, here she was alone, further than she had ever been from the village, and it was getting dark.

The clouds, which had been gathering all day, now hung thick and threatening, but the rain held off. Adjusting the bag onto her shoulder one more time, she bit her lip and began to walk faster. She pushed against the dusk till finally the trees parted, and she saw the house. Even in the gathering dark, she could make out the outline of an immense mansion looming before her—a colossal building that was considered the closest thing this region had to a palace.

She paused. There were no lights. Was something wrong?

It was starting to rain hard—mammoth drops of water. Not a good sign. It would soon be a downpour.

Anna ran the rest of the way and pounded on the massive oak door. There was no movement. She opened the door. It was silent. Why hadn't the man lit his lamps? What mood would he be in now with a thunderstorm pending?

As the door opened wide, she could smell the sweetish, rotting smell that lingers in a derelict building. Obviously, Boris wasn't at home much these days. The interior of this house continued to amaze her. Even though it was completely neglected, it still had remnants of its former glory. It was as wild and crazy as the owner, a man who had once thought he could transform an old mansion-like house into a winter palace.

This was a man who loved red. "Red commands attention and provides stimulation, like fireworks exploding in the sky," he said. He loved anything that exploded, and his house was an explosion of colors. But now it was dark....

Anna paused. “Anyone home?” she called out. “Boris Balakirev are you home?” There was no answer.

Then she heard barking. She opened the front door. Canon, the dog, came rushing around the corner of the house, barking aggressively and angrily till he recognized her and stopped short. Delighted to see her, Canon began to jump up on her, wagging his tail furiously. She slipped him a piece of stale roast beef she had brought just for him.

She found an old gas lamp that she lit with a match. When it sputtered to life, it cast a flickering light over the peeling wallpaper and threadbare carpet of a long, gloomy front hallway where a candle chandelier covered with cobwebs still hung overhead.

She called out again. There was no answer. Outside it was beginning to thunder. Lightning soon followed. She continued to shiver from exhaustion, from her pain, her wet clothes and now the coolness of the house.

Taking the lamp, she slowly began to inspect the house with Canon at her side. It was truly deserted. The parlor looked as if it hadn’t been used for some time; the bedrooms with their rumpled bedcovers were empty; and the kitchen had the usual mounds of dishes stacked on every available counter space.

But there was fresh wood in every fireplace, a sign that Boris had been here recently, and judging from the ashtrays, his pipes—and the cups of coffee—he had been here this morning. Probably he hadn’t arrived home yet from the fields, she decided. He wasn’t a man who kept track of the time. The evening darkness might have caught him off guard.

The one likely place she hadn't check yet was the library. The door was closed. This was the sanctuary of the house. This was the one room that was usually looked after.

Anna opened the door. The musty smell of old books filled the room—and she savored it. Nothing had changed; the walls were lined with floor to ceiling wooden shelves filled with hundreds of books. On the floor, pillars of books were stacked four feet high at least. And on top of these books, there were open books, lying on their spines, half read—waiting to be finished. The movement of the books was current. Boris was still around.

Anna smiled to herself. This was where she would wait for him. If only her mother were here to share this moment.

The first thing she needed to do was flood the room with light. She went around the room to light all the lamps. She already knew that this was the only room where the lamps were tended, ready to be lit. Once the room was flooded with light, Anna lit the fire in the fireplace. There was plenty of wood. With Canon keeping her company she felt safer than she had for a long time.

Then she found blankets. She moved a lumpy wing-backed chair close to the fire, pulled a pillow from one of the corners, found a new book, and sat down. She took an apple from her bag.

Canon lay down at her feet, his eyes on the fire. She loved the room; even the faded velvet drapes didn't matter, nor the dirty tapestry hanging on the one wall that wasn't covered with books. She loved it all. The rain drumming on the windows was comforting.

Slowly she could feel her trembling ease as the blanket warmed her and the throbbing in her shoulder became bearable. She could feel the weariness melt into a deep yearning to sleep.

Once before when she had come here with her mother, and they had waited under the trees for Boris, he had scolded them for not going inside and making themselves comfortable. "I leave my doors open so my friends can come whenever they wish. My dogs take care of my enemies," he had said with a laugh. And they did. Canon, so friendly and so obedient, could be vicious with a stranger. He could lead his pack against any formidable foe. She was thankful he considered her a friend.

She began to munch on her apple. The book was a new one by Lidia Zinovieva-Annibal, *The Tragic Menagerie*. Anna lost herself in the words of the book. It didn't matter now that it was storming outside, that she was in a strange home and didn't know where the owner was. She had escaped into another world.

Chapter EIGHT

"Follow me," Boris said, his eyes glowing. "I know a short cut. We can get to the house before it pours."

Without waiting for an answer, Boris spurred his horse into a run. Johann followed at a full gallop.

They didn't make it. They were still quite a distance from the house when the torrential rain began to pour down on them. Yet Boris didn't stop; instead, he seemed even more invigorated. He whooped with joy—wielding his gun and shooting at anything that moved. He led the race home—his jacket flapping wildly in the storm.

Johann couldn't believe the man. Eccentric, touched in the head, perhaps even a little dangerous—he wasn't quite sure how he would describe this Boris Balakirev. The only thing he knew was that he needed to follow this man, because if he didn't, he wasn't sure he would find his way out of this wilderness of a farm.

Because he had heard that Boris wanted to sell the property, they had spent the entire day riding the farm. From what he had seen, this estate had exciting possibilities.

What he liked most was that it was close to the Kuban River—and only a few versts out of the Kuban village, closer to Olginskoye, and not that far from the railway. More and more Mennonites were finding that they could exercise a bit more freedom living outside the confines of the village. Estates were springing up as quickly and as suddenly as mushrooms after a rain. It was a sign of the growing confidence in the economic stability of the southern colonies. There were some drawbacks to living outside the safety of the community; one was the need to hire one's own security. But that could be managed easily. Security guards could always double as farm help.

Johann had been favorably impressed all day. The rundown state of the farm would keep the asking price low. The bones were good. The trees around the house were magnificent. The fences—those that still existed—were stable. The rocks had been gathered and piled along the fences. There were two lagoons, one out in the pasture, and one closer to the house. The well was good. The sheds were in a dreadful state. There were two barns, one barn might have to be demolished because the roof had a dangerous swayback. All in all, it would be a lot of work. The farm was definitely overgrown with weeds and brush, but all of that could be dealt with in time.

And he did have time.... He had time to research this farm, the Kuban villages and the Rempel family. He was mainly interested in learning more about Rempel.

He had never been close to his father but had immediately taken to this amazing business man who was somehow able to straddle the Mennonite and Russian cultures in a way he had never seen a Mennonite do before. During Rempel's visit to the mother colonies, he had invited Johann to the Kuban villages to explore business possibilities—a mentorship of sorts—which is why he was here. He wanted to watch Rempel and learn.

He didn't realize that Rempel had another agenda—and that was for him to meet his two daughters, Beth and Rina. At first, he hadn't been interested but now was enjoying being part of the family—with Sunday faspas and playing crokinole in the evenings. He always won and Beth came in second. He was finding her quite delightful.

Closer to the house, Boris slowed down. It was Boris' habit to approach his house slowly and stealthily—one never knew who might have arrived, or what their intentions might be. At the edge of the yard, Boris slid off his horse. Johann did the same.

"We have visitors," Boris said. There was a light in one of the windows. "Canon is with them. This could be good—or not so good."

They took their time to rub down the horses, feed them, and look after the rest of the animals in the barn. There were a few pigs, chickens, cats and sheep.

When they were finished, Boris went to the door of the barn. It was still raining. "Now let's see who our visitors are. After we look after them, we'll have supper—and then you can camp in one of the many bedrooms for the night. It's no problem for me. In the morning we can look at the yard more closely."

Johann nodded. He had told Neufeld not to expect him. It was probably just as well; Neufeld's home, though hospitable, was tiny. To find lodging somewhere else, even for a night, would be a kind of relief. That was why he needed to find a place for himself. He would like one more look at the farm in the morning and then he would make up his mind. The more time he could spend here the more he would know—which meant fewer surprises later on.

Pulling their jackets over their heads, they dashed for the house. But once at the house, Boris put his finger to his lips, Johann nodded.

Stealthily they opened the door, and without lighting a lamp they groped their way through the first rooms to the room with the light.

Just as they were about to open the door, they heard a bark. Swinging his ever-present rifle onto his shoulder, Boris threw open the door and exploded into the room.

Johann followed cautiously. It was a sight he would never forget. There was a big, black dog moving towards them, his wide tail wagging furiously, bouncing and jumping on his master. Behind the dog, sitting in a massive, wingback chair was a young woman. Her hair, a smoky auburn, naturally tightly curled from the damp air, rose like a tangled halo over her head. She was a vision of beauty, breathtaking. Quiet but alarmed, she sat there, book in hand, waiting—waiting for the rifle to be put down. There was a fire blazing in the fireplace, making the room warm and welcoming.

Boris threw down his rifle, and opened his arms. "Anna," he said. The woman rose to her feet. She was tall, thin. When she allowed the blankets to fall, he saw that she was dressed in a simple cotton dress. She ran into the man's arms. "Boris! You do know how to scare me half to death."

Canon was jumping all around them, creating a kind of chaos that Johann had rarely seen.

"I am so sorry I frightened you. Let me look at you. I haven't seen you enough. You are shaking like a leaf." Boris held her at arm's length.

Anna laughed. "It's not often that I have a gun pointed at me."

They laughed together like old friends.

"I am so sorry." Boris paused. "Forgive me. I am a dreadful host. You must know Johann Baerg."

Anna felt giddy with relief at seeing Boris; she had hardly noticed the man behind him. Exceptionally handsome, dark shaggy hair and cool blue eyes. Interesting eyes, she mused, an intelligent blue. She remembered the name. This was the man who intended to move from the mother colonies to live here in the Kuban villages and was staying with the Neufelds until he bought a farm. He was also a guest of the Rempels—which would suggest that he was interested in Beth—the most sought-after girl in the villages.

"And Johann, this is Anna." Boris was smiling broadly, as he kept his arm around her. "Anna is the one Mennonite I know who shares my interest in Russian literature."

"Anna?" The name swam through his mind, and his gut clenched. This was—the Mayor 's daughter—who was being considered for excommunication because of her dangerous interest in world literature. Slowly he became aware of the décor—piles of books stacked in the shelves and on the floor. He surveyed the room again; he saw the open book by the fireplace. He had just caught her in the forbidden act.

Anna read his thoughts. She saw his eyes harden, and knew she had been found out. This man was part of the church council. He had just caught her red-handed.

He could see the blood drain from her face, as the realization of who he was, and what he represented dawned on her.

Boris was oblivious to the growing tension between them. "We are going to have a lovely evening. Both of you must stay the night—I have room. And I have food. We are all famished, I'm sure. I am usually lonely. Now I have two exquisite guests." He started towards the door. "I will start supper immediately."

"No, don't bother. Not to worry," Anna quickly said. "I have brought us a wonderful supper, and I'm sure there is plenty for three. Why don't we just have it here in the library? You must be tired—out and about all day?"

"Yes," Boris enthused. "Johann has been examining my farm. He is considering buying it. Isn't that good news? I am ready for a rest." With that, he began to move furniture around. Johann helped him clear a table of books, bringing together three chairs around the fire. Canon was following him around, obviously happy to be in the house with his master.

As Anna watched Boris, she tried to think through what he had just said. She was in shock. No, it wasn't good news at all, she thought, that he was going to sell this wonderful, mysterious, treasure-filled house. It was another loss. She was losing her mother, bit by bit—till she would have nothing left, of herself, or of her memories. She wasn't ready for this. She wasn't ready to leave the literature. She still needed to know.... She needed time.... She bit her lower lip. If this house was taken from her, it could mean losing everything. Outside she could hear the thunder and lightning unleash its full fury on the earth.

When the furniture was arranged, Anna opened her bag and began to unpack and set up the food. She was glad that she had brought extra. The men were obviously hungry. Boris rarely thought of food during the day, and was famished in the evenings. Once the table was set, Boris paused.

"Johann, would you say grace?" Boris had lived among Mennonites long enough to know their customs.

Johann lowered his head, and said a short prayer, thanking God for the gracious host, for the good day, for the rain, and for the food. He did not mention her. Anna was keenly aware of the omission, knowing it was probably deliberate. It was the beginning of the shunning, recognizing neither her presence nor her contribution. She could feel her temperature rise. She kept her eyes fastened on the food. This was too humiliating for words. Why had he come? Why had he wrecked her perfect visit with this wonderful friend?

Boris remained oblivious. "This food is wonderful," he said, plunging in with almost barbaric delight. They were silent as they concentrated on the food. The rain was beginning to come down like nothing she had ever heard before. It pounded on the windows as if it would break them. Boris took no notice of it at all.

Finally, taking a break from the sausage and buns, he reached around to the open book that Anna had been reading. "Hmm, Lidia Zinovieva-Annibal, *The Tragic Menagerie.* I notice that you found my newest book. What do you think of it, Anna?" Anna could feel her color rise.

"I hardly had a chance to read before I was rushed by a mad man with a gun," she said with a warm smile. "And that moment has just wiped my mind clean. What did you think of it?"

It was the opening that he had been waiting for—to talk about his books. Next to reading the books herself, listening to him talk about them was her next most treasured time. So she leaned back; the room was warm now, his voice mellow. If she ignored the man, Johann, sitting to her left, she could even enjoy the moment.

Johann could not take his eyes off her. All his life he had been warned against people who were not God-followers—especially those in the church. To become entangled with one was as dangerous as drinking, smoking or dancing. Here was one of them obviously flaunting Mennonite traditions. She was indulging in literature that had been banned by the elders;

yet he couldn't help being intrigued. Even now, as she leaned back, her eyes riveted on the man Boris, she was obviously enjoying the words at a level he could not understand.

She was beautiful.

He needed to remain aloof, he decided. He would endure the evening, endure their presence, continue to research the farm, and then once he bought the farm, he would have to do much work to change all of this. He would have to purge the house, the land……

Boris suddenly jumped up. "I am remiss as a host. You must have some of my hospitality drink."

Anna smiled. She knew what was coming. Boris had a "fruit juice" that he insisted everyone partake of. He was quite upset if his guests refused. Very early on in their visits they had realized this, and her mother had always indulged him. Actually, this juice made one feel all warm and comfortable so they had never asked about its contents. They didn't know what was in it, and Boris had never explained.

In no time Boris was back with three glasses. "Here," he said. "We will toast to new beginnings—Johann coming here, buying the farm, Anna—your new life, and mine."

Anna was about to ask what her "new life" meant but she knew he was just being kind. She took a sip of her drink. True to its reputation, she felt a warmth fill her body that was delicious and comforting.

She glanced at Johann. He had no idea what he was drinking. Fruit juice was acceptable; the name was acceptable. He was sipping it slowly, tasting it, thinking about it. "This is good," he finally said.

Boris broke into a smile. He was now satisfied. He kept their glasses full.

Outside, the fierceness of the storm had abated.

"We need music," he said, taking out an old guitar. Then with relish he played a few songs, singing some of the old Russian ballads for them.

The food, the music, the juice, being surrounded by old books, good words, the acceptance by this funny man, the dog at her feet, Anna could think of nothing more sensuous and soul satisfying. Her mother would have loved it. That had been the interesting part of her mother. Her mother loved the stiff formal church liturgy as well as wild, creative beauty. She was able to embrace different worlds.... Why was that not allowed?

She noticed that Johann was leaning back in his chair, enjoying the moment, though probably denying it in his heart. There was something about him that intrigued her. He was self-assured, so confident. She had heard that he was wealthy and highly skilled. She envied him, his comfort in the established church.

He was handsome.

Then she smiled. She could now tell the elders that Johann had been caught drinking. She could embarrass him good. But what would be the point?

Boris laid down the guitar. Then settling into his chair, he began to tell his stories. Now that he had a captive audience, mellowed to the point of dozing—he could talk—and talk he did. He told them his entire life story—his trips to St.

Petersburg, his time abroad, the wars and the people he had met—and then about the books. It was always about the books.

"I'm writing a book," he said. And this was to be the climax of the evening, but both of his guests were nodding off. "But we'll have to save that for another night." He looked at the two of them, so quiet—both struggling against sleep. And he couldn't stop smiling.

Chapter NINE

She flung off her covers, and stretched luxuriously. She hadn't slept so soundly for a long time. She vaguely remembered being carried to bed after falling asleep to the sound of Boris' storytelling voice, being covered with blanket and then sinking into the softness and serenity of a perfect rest.

She slipped out of bed and went to the bulging closet. She and Nadia and her mother, when they had stayed over, had always helped themselves to the dresses that were left here by all the other women who had lived here before. There was a large selection of every kind of dress—plain to gaudy. This time she chose a moss green dress of raw silk with delicate pearl buttons down the front. It fit her perfectly. She would wear it and save her own dresses from getting dirty as she cleaned the house.

From a wooden jewelry box on the dresser, she chose a matching pearl hair clip. Unhappy with her frizzed hair reflected in the gilded mirror, she tried to braid it but it was completely unmanageable; so, she swept it up into a loose topknot, allowing tendrils of curls to frame her face. She actually liked the change. She didn't appear so severe. This was so much fun. If only Nadia and her mother were here to enjoy this with her.

By the time she reached the kitchen the men were already looking for something to eat in the pantry. She pulled out the leftovers of their supper from the night before. They ate some of the sausage, buns and cheese, then the men quickly left to do chores and to continue their tour of the farm.

Ordinarily, she would have been tempted to go back to the library and read, but for the first time she didn't want to escape the Saturday morning chores, she wanted to transform this house into a home.

She hauled in pails of water and tackled the mounds of dishes. Then she checked the pantry and was surprised that though neglected, it was stocked with flour and the essentials. There were even some leftover jars of vegetable preserves. Boris must have someone coming in occasionally. This was just enough to make the men a good lunch that might even cover supper.

She had been taught to do much with little; this would not even be a challenge. In no time, she had buns rising near the stove, and a pot of borscht cooking on the back burner of the big stove.

The mood of the kitchen changed immediately and drastically. Anna smiled to herself as she surveyed the kitchen; her work was cut out for her. Already the house smelled of rising dough and borscht.

After the kitchen was transformed, she decided to air the musty quilts. But where to put them? She had never explored the yard. Was there even a wash line? Was there anything to hang them on—even a fence?

She stepped outside. The backyard was different than what she was used to. Most of the yard was unkempt, except for an enclosed garden to the side of the house that was almost hidden from view—which looked inviting. Another hint that Boris was hiring some kind of help.

Anna slowly opened the broken garden gate. It was obvious that at one time the backyard had been a lovely garden. Huge spruce trees bordered the north side of the garden; lilac bushes and other ornamental shrubs bordered the east side. And it was all enclosed by a crumbling rock fence that was barely visible under a runaway rambling rose bush. There were scattered fields of forget-me-nots, buttercups and white daisies under the trees. In the middle, the only place where the sun could shine, there were islands of peonies and daffodils growing wild amidst patches of tall grasses. The vegetable garden in the corner plot was dismal but functioning.

There was no clothesline, only a remnant pole with a tiny little hook. There was some rope that she could string from one tree to the next. It all had potential.

Anna was about to fetch the first blanket when she heard the sound of galloping horses. She ran into the front yard. In the distance, she could see two horses galloping towards her, the first ahead of the second.

The dogs, led by Canon, immediately came running from the barn, barking wildly.

Boris, gun in hand, came charging out of the barn yelling and whooping at the top of his voice, firing warning shots. Johann was right after him, yelling for Boris to stop. Had Boris gone mad?

Then Anna recognized the riders. "It's Aaron and Jakob," she screamed, hoping Boris would recognize them. "My brothers."

Boris went down on one knee and aimed his gun again. In his state of mind, every galloping rider was an armed enemy.

"Boris, don't!" Anna screamed again, running towards him. "It's my brothers. Stop, don't shoot!" Would Boris even recognize her in his madness?

She threw herself on top of him. Boris fell over, cursing loudly, still wildly shooting the gun. Briefly, it pointed at her.

"Boris, it's me, Anna!"

Slowly, painfully slow, he put the gun down. "You shouldn't do that, Anna. You could get us both killed."

"Boris, I had to. It's Aaron, my brother and Jakob, my stepbrother."

"Then we need to greet them properly," Boris smiled, got up and walked towards the horses.

The dogs continued their barking as the first horse came galloping into the yard and stopping at the main door. Aaron's horse reared with fright at the commotion and for a minute,

Anna thought Aaron would be bucked off, but he hung on, and then slid off.

The second horse was trotting slower. They noticed that it had two riders—Jakob and a passenger.

"Anna," Jakob called. "I need your help. It's Nadia. She's been hurt."

Anna ran toward him, but before she could reach him, Nadia fell off the horse and into a puddle—a massive puddle left from last night's downpour. Anna reached her first—knelt down beside the girl, pushing back the black hair that had fallen over her face. Anna recoiled in horror. There was an open, angry gash across her cheek, swollen purplish bruises around her eyes and a maze of scratches on every part of exposed skin. The girl was almost unrecognizable. Anna slipped off her shawl and wrapped it around Nadia.

"Who did this to her?" Anna gasped, looking up at Jakob. "Where did you find her?" Anna tried to help Nadia to her feet, but she sank back. Nadia couldn't stand up.

Jakob slid off his horse and tied it to the hitching post. He was grinning. "Looks like a mess—doesn't she?"

Anna tried to ignore his cruel smile. He was Widow Wieler's oldest son, a little older than herself, which had made their relationship a little awkward right from the beginning when he had moved into their house. At one point, he had tried to strike up a relationship with her but she had found him disgusting with his crude jokes, his arrogance and condescending attitude towards the servants. Sometimes she wondered if her stepparents were punishing her for this rejection by keeping her isolated from all other possible suitors.

Kneeling in the puddle, Anna slipped an arm around Nadia as she moaned again. Her eyes rolled slowly as she lost consciousness again. "We need to get her inside."

Johann stepped forward, and with very little effort, he picked Nadia up in his arms and carried her into the house as if she were as light as a feather. Aaron followed him.

Jakob continued to chuckle. "She's a mess. Could barely hang on the whole way. Kept whimpering about being scared…."

"What happened to her? Who would do something like this?" Anna asked.

He shook his head. "Don't know what's happened. Everyone in town is looking for Nadia. All I know if that I better get back and tell them that she's safe so they can stop wasting their time. I'll let them know that you are all safe here."

He chuckled again as he swung onto his horse. "Aaron can help with Nadia. And with Boris shooting at everything, you'll be safe here, I'm sure." Then with an unenthusiastic wave, he turned his horse and galloped down the lane, pushing his tired horse to its limits.

With Aaron's help, Johann carried Nadia up the back stairs into the kitchen, down the hall, and into a small spare bedroom on the main floor, depositing her on the bed. Anna followed him. Nadia was beginning to shiver uncontrollably.

The minute he laid her on the bed, Anna began to peel off her wet outer clothes. "Need to get these off so she can warm up," she muttered.

Johann nodded. "I looked after my father when he had an accident," he said as he quickly examined her. "Nothing appears to be broken," he said, "except maybe her ribs." He touched her gently and she flinched violently. 'Can't do much for that—just know she's in a lot of pain."

"What do you think happened?"

"A beating," he said.

It did look like a beating, Anna thought. The ghastly wounds looked like the result of the harshest, most brutal beating Anna had ever seen. Surely Widow Wieler couldn't have managed this? Anna felt her blood turn to ice. But who else would do this? Had Mikhail Kamensky?

Johann rolled up his sleeves. "I'll need bandages, hot water, wash cloths—a glass of water—perhaps a glass of that famous juice. It might ease her pain," Johann said.

"Shouldn't we get a doctor?" Anna asked.

Nadia came out of the stupor long enough to shake her head vehemently, then grimaced with pain. "No doctor," she said. "Please, no doctor. Just rest."

Anna went back to the kitchen for hot water, and more towels. She asked Boris for his first aid supplies that he had used during the war. He disappeared into his pantry and emerged with an old wooden box filled with dusty bottles and bandages. When Anna returned to the room with the supplies, Johann took them from her. Then carefully, he washed the wounds, covered them with ointment and bandaged them with a doctor's skill. Meanwhile Anna gave the wounded body a sponge bath, cleaning the mud off as best she could.

Finally, holding her in a sitting position, Johann helped Nadia take some of Boris' famous juice.

Leaning back against the pillows, Nadia murmured her thank you repeatedly through swollen lips.

"Is there anything else you need?"

Nadia shook her head.

He stroked her hand. "Rest now," he said. "You are safe here."

Anna had never seen anyone handle another person's wounds so gently, so professionally.

"I want to thank you, too, for looking after my friend," she said to him as they left the room together. "Nadia is special to me."

He only nodded.

In the kitchen, Aaron and Boris were sitting at the table helping themselves to the borscht and coffee.

Anna slipped a pan of the rising buns into the oven.

Boris smiled. "Anna—you are a miracle worker. My kitchen has never looked so good. And this borscht—out of nothing—so quickly—it is a miracle."

"Looks as if you do have help coming in but you need a full-time maid, Boris—to look after you."

"Nadia can do that," Boris said, continuing to grin. "Nadia should stay with me now…. Maybe she will."

Johann noticed a shadow fall over Anna's face and knew there was something else behind the banter.

He sat down at the kitchen table by the window and looked out into the yard. More than anything he wanted to be out there—touring the estate. Even now as he looked out at the neglected garden, he could see that it had a wild beauty, but nothing in comparison to what it could look like with a little care and maintenance. He wanted to get out there and continue to examine this farm—make an offer. But something was going on here. Something dangerous....

Anna set a cup of coffee down in front of him. "Would you like to have a bowl of borscht now—or wait until the buns are baked?"

"I'll wait," he said.

She seemed pleased with his answer.

Then she sat down opposite Aaron. "Now tell me what happened," she said.

Aaron shoved his empty bowl away. "After you left. I went to do chores—I noticed this strange horse and was coming in to ask about it when I saw Nadia being kidnapped by three goons. Then I noticed that someone was in the house. I knew you had left. Nadia was in trouble. So I grabbed a stick and ran into the house to find this man—a Russian officer—sitting and dozing in the parlor. He woke up with a start and was as confused as I was. We had a quick chat.... Then Jakob and I went chasing after the kidnappers while Kamensky stayed back to wait for the family. We didn't find her and came back late at night in the middle of that wicked storm to find our father and mother talking to Kamensky. Then it was his turn to go and look—he said that he thought he had some leads. So he went out into the storm to go look.

We all went to bed. I'm not sure when Kamensky came back. But he was there for breakfast. He was really worried about you—Anna. He let us know that Nadia had been left in a shed not that far from here—so Jakob and I were sent to go find her and help her. But actually, Kamensky wasn't that concerned about Nadia—he was more concerned about you. He wanted us to know in the worst way where you were. He kind of hinted that you were the target…"

Aaron took a sip of his coffee. "I was told by our parents—they made it very clear that we all were to protect your whereabouts. But I'm under strict orders now to bring you back with me. We don't have much time. I'm not sure we should even wait for the buns. I need to take you back, Anna."

Anna paused. "What do you mean? I'm staying here for another two days."

"Oh no, you're not. Gertrude and Abram will be upset. You know how they feel about Boris—his books and you."

"I'm staying here," she repeated. "Nadia needs me here." She seemed extremely agitated. She bent over the oven to check the buns.

Then she began to putter around the kitchen. Johann watched her take the milk pail that they had brought in from the barn and strain the liquid through a piece of white cloth. She was working automatically—not thinking. She placed the milk on the table. Her fingers were trembling.

Aaron became agitated when Anna would not budge.

Johann watched both of them as he took a sip of his coffee. It was good coffee. This girl could do wonders in a kitchen. Even in that awful Russian dress, she looked lovely as she continued to bring order to the kitchen and serve them.

"We need to go," Aaron kept saying. "We're already in heaps of trouble. Getrude and Abram are now convinced that you are in danger—and could be beaten like Nadia. And that you now need to talk to Kamensky. They now believe it was wrong to keep you from talking to him. They don't know what this is all about. But they want you home tonight for his reception!"

"How did all this start?" Johann asked calmly, not sure he should get involved, aching to be gone himself. "I think we all need to know. Start from the beginning. Tell me what you know. Start from the beginning again."

"Beginning?" Aaron glanced at his sister. "I don't even know when this all started. I think it probably started with you Anna. Why did you fool Mikhail? Why did you pretend to be Nadia and Nadia you? That's how this all started."

Anna threw up her hands. "Don't blame this on me. I was told not to introduce myself or talk to Mikhail. That wasn't my choice. The Mayor received a letter from Mikhail Kamensky asking to see me—or someone known as Anna. The Mayor and the Widow did not want me to talk to him. so when he came a day early, and I was the only one home, I didn't lie. I just pretended that I needed to find a family member." She was noticeably flushed and agitated.

"That's when I came to the fields looking for you—but you were sleeping and grumpy. I asked Nadia to keep Kamensky amused. I packed up some food and left to come here. I thought Widow Wieler would be happy that I didn't talk to this Kamensky person—and that Nadia had dealt with it."

"Nadia?" Johann asked, still puzzled.

Aaron sighed. "Apparently, Nadia introduced herself as Anna to Mikhail, and then when she went to the backyard, there were three riders who grabbed her and rode off with her into the night. I saw it happen and ran into the house, thought Mikhail was an intruder, and nearly killed him."

Anna pulled the buns out of the oven. The aroma of fresh baking filled the kitchen. She let the buns slide onto a plate and put it on the table. She brought a bowl of jam. Then she sat down to drink her coffee. "I still don't understand the part about Nadia being taken."

"No one does. She won't talk. Both Jakob and I tried to ask her questions, but she wouldn't even try to answer them."

"Do you think it has something to do with her pretending to be me?"

Aaron shrugged.

Johann watched them closely. Were they just not telling all or were they genuinely confused? These were the Mayor's stepchildren who were causing their parents such anxiety. These were the parents who wanted them excommunicated from the church. But why the abduction? Why not let Anna talk to Mikhail? Why the switch? Why the beating? And why didn't Anna want to go home? Why would she rather stay and fix up this dilapidated old house, look after this crazy man and the wounded servant than go home?

Boris was watching them too. "I'll beat up the bastards when we find them. Then I'll shoot them," he said, filling up his bowl with borscht again and helping himself to the buns smearing them with jam.

Boris leaned back. This time his eyes were focused. "Anna—this is all about you. What do you have that someone like Mikhail Kamensky would want—that the Tsar would want?"

Anna shook her head. "I don't have anything. The Tsar doesn't know I exist. Aaron and I have no connections—no living family. We are really orphans living at the Mayor's house. And he and his wife hate us." Her voice was desperate. "I just don't want to go back there –especially now with all of this."

Johann felt her pleading eyes seek his. He could always sense and feel fear. He respected fear. He was starting to understand….

"Maybe it's the pin you wear?" Aaron said.

"Pin—what pin?" Boris asked.

"Aaron!" Anna exclaimed. "You aren't supposed to talk about the pin."

"What pin?" Johann asked.

"Mikhail saw it, Anna. He wondered about it too. He recognized it, and said it was a Fabergé brooch," Aaron continued. "I saw something in his eyes…. It raised suspicion."

"Fabergé brooch? Do you have it here?" Boris asked, suddenly very alert.

Anna nodded. She turned away from them and removed it from her collar. Then turned back, holding it in the palm of her hand.

Boris took a quick look at it. "Fabergé all right. Can recognize their work from a mile away. It would fetch some money but not enough to cause this kind of stir. Why not just steal the pin?" He shook his head in disgust.

"Can I see it?" Johann asked.

Anna didn't want to give it to him. The church was not to know about the jewelry her mother had given to her. They frowned upon anything that hinted of pride in one's appearance or wealth. Yet—she owed Johann, for looking after Nadia so tenderly.

Reluctantly Anna gave it to him. He bent over to examine it. If only Johann wasn't here. His dark, scathing looks had unnerved her completely last night. She knew exactly what he was thinking. And this morning nothing had changed; in fact, it had intensified. Now it was as if the entire church council had somehow inhabited his eyes. It was the last thing she needed.... The church to be judging her at this moment.

"Not many people know I have this pin. I don't wear it to enhance my appearance," she explained cautiously. "I treasure it because it is so beautiful and it was a gift from my mother. It reminds me of her."

"I won't tell anyone about it." He gave it back. He had heard about this Fabergé jewelry. Even he could tell that this piece of jewelry was truly exquisite. It was a rare brooch, two large green enameled leaves with a ribboned wreath, containing one cabochon sapphire circled with diamonds and set against a gold background.

"Can I see it again?" Boris asked.

Boris examined it closely." It is Fabergé," he said. "When I was at the Winter Palace, I met Peter Carl Fabergé, the well-known court jeweler. It was before Easter and he was showing a few people one of the eggs that he had prepared for the Imperial family's Easter tradition that year. It was remarkable. He was commissioned to make an egg a year." He gave the brooch back to Anna. "It is beautiful. I can see why you treasure it."

Johann turned to Boris. "You don't think that brooch is worthy of this fuss?"

Boris shook his head. "It would fetch some money, to be sure, but not enough for the Tsar's people to come looking for it. Something's afoot." He turned to Anna. "You sure you don't have more of these?"

Anna looked shocked. "Never! How would my mother have access to such?"

"How did she come to own that piece?" Johann asked. He looked from one to the other. Both Anna and Aaron shrugged.

Johann hated to get involved but he couldn't help it. "Anna, I think you need to go back to the village. There is something going on—and you need to go back where you will be safe."

"Safe?" Anna's eyes were large.

Johann had always been taught to look after the members of the congregation. Even though he would have preferred to go out and spend the rest of this beautiful day riding the estate, he knew as a church council member that he had some obligation here. "I will come with you to your parents and explain everything. Nothing will harm you when I am with you," Johann said.

She finally nodded.

"I don't see why you have to leave…." Boris said mournfully.

A voice from the door in the hallway intruded into their conversation. "If you leave, I'm going—with you."

Everyone turned. Nadia was standing in the doorway, wearing a robe, looking as if she could hardly focus her eyes, much less stand. "I have to—go with you," she said, breathing heavily.

Boris stood up. "I forbid it. Look at you. You're not fit to travel—and no one can protect you like I can."

"I'm staying with Anna," Nadia said, taking gulps. "There is nothing—you can do—to persuade me—otherwise."

"But you are in such pain." Anna rose to put her arm around Nadia. "I should be staying here to look after you."

Nadia shook her head. "No—you need to go back to—the village—and I need to go—with you."

Johann sighed. "It looks as if we all need to go back. We have only two horses and there are four of us going back. Perhaps, if we borrowed your buggy, Boris?"

"Yes." Boris looked sad and dejected. "You may use it. I just don't want any of you to go. This was going so well."

Johann stood up. "Then we need to start back immediately. Sorry, Boris—would love to have stayed one more day."

Anna helped Nadia back to her room to dress.

Boris pressured Johann to make a decision about the farm, but Johann resisted. "I need to see it one more day," he kept saying.

Boris was most particularly disappointed that Anna was going back." We haven't talked," he kept saying. "You haven't had a chance to look at the books."

She nodded, very aware that Johann was watching them closely. He could use this against her—this literature bond between her and Boris. She was tempted to tell Boris that her interest had waned, to make a public confession and turnabout just for Johann's sake, but the words stuck in her throat. She couldn't change—not just because the church said so. She needed more than that. She needed to be convinced that what she was doing was truly wrong—and that God disapproved. But she didn't feel that. The literature didn't take her away from her God. In fact, it strengthened her faith. She was learning that true literature was about the struggle of good and evil. It was always about God. Her mother had told her once that if one was a true believer in God, there was nothing that could dissuade one from that. To glimpse God once was to see God in everything and in everyone. Even in the seemingly meaningless ramblings in literature, there was always a presence of God if one knew where to look.

"I will be back, Boris," she said loudly enough for Johann to hear. "I can't take any books this time. We are going into summer and you know how busy it is, and how I can't resist a good book. But I will be back in fall. Thank you so much for everything."

"Thank you, Anna," Boris said, with tears in his eyes. "You are your mother's daughter."

He couldn't have said anything sweeter to her; so, she hugged him tightly.

"Take care of yourself," she whispered to him. And she meant it more than anything in the world.

Aaron was relieved to be going back. His mission had been accomplished. "They need to know that Nadia and Anna are both safe," he kept saying to himself.

By the time they left, it was three o'clock in the afternoon. With the sway of the buggy, the warm sun on their faces, it was no time at all before both Nadia and Aaron were fast asleep.

Anna couldn't sleep. Nadia had laid her head on her lap. She still couldn't take her eyes off her face with its bruises and cuts. Who would do something like this?

But there was something else that worried Anna; something had changed in Nadia. For the first while, Anna had tried to ask Nadia about the beating, but Nadia had been evasive. She didn't want to talk about it, which for Anna meant that she was still frightened. All Anna had found out was that there had been three of them—and Mikhail Kamensky had not been one of them.

With both Aaron and Nadia sleeping, she would have enjoyed a conversation with Johann to find out where he had learned his skill in nursing, what his interests were in the farm. She had been impressed with the way he had handled Nadia and the fact that he was willing to give up his desire to stay behind and assess the estate—all to help them get back to the village. She was intrigued… interested in him … admired him. Of all the men she had met—he was the most complex and worthy….

Yet she still could feel his disapproval. She would not let her mind wander….

Uncomfortable in the buggy with the strain between them, she yearned to go back to the big house. Someday she would find a way to live in a house like that.

Johann remained alert. He was very aware that somewhere very close to Boris' estate, they had picked up a tail. Someone was following them.

If nothing else, this tail convinced him that they were doing the right thing by going back to the village. The mystery needed to be solved. What intrigued him was Boris' reaction to and interest in the Fabergé pin. Why had he connected the name Mikhail Kamensky immediately with the Tsar? That man knew more than he let on.

Johann still wasn't clear on his thoughts about the Franz children, especially Anna. She was a disturbing presence, a contradiction. She seemed to be so loving, beautiful—yet she had this incredible, dark interest in Russian culture. It didn't make sense to him. Yet there was something about her....

Chapter TEN

Mikhail watched the man squirm. In any other village, he'd take this man to the outskirts of the village and force the information out of him; but he couldn't do things like that now that he had been introduced as representing the Tsar in an official capacity.

This was one visit that he needed to complete before he investigated Anna again. While the family was preparing for the gala—he had decided to visit Loepky in his home.

"I'm here to investigate why your church, a Mennonite church in good standing, can't raise the money for their taxes. All the other denominations in this village have been compliant, except for this church. Your members are contributing—at least that's what they are reporting to the Mayor—but the church accountant does not have enough money. The membership, contributions and balance aren't adding up. Schellenberg tells me that some members go to him to pay their taxes—which makes sense, he is the church treasurer—but for some reason, others go to you. The rich on the estates seem to prefer to go to you. He does not accuse you; he swears that you are an honest pastor. I'm not convinced. I need an explanation."

Mikhail watched under hooded eyes. The man was guilty. He had also heard from Schellenberg that Loepky wanted in the worst way to move to America. Mikhail suspected that was where the money was going. The stallion that had been stolen had apparently been from Rempel, a rich recluse living on an estate. This holy man was wheeling and dealing. This holy man was probably not so holy.

"Are you calling me a liar?" Loepky asked with indignation, a flush of hurt innocence flooding his eyes.

Mikhail nodded. The innocent act might have been convincing to someone less sophisticated in the art of espionage, but he could see right through it. This man's holy indignation didn't wash. He was protesting too much. "In fact, I have proof," Mikhail said. The man blanched. Inwardly Mikhail smiled. The man was exactly where he wanted him, weak with guilt and fear. Mikhail leaned forward. "But I will look the other way because I have an offer for you…."

Loepky raided his eyebrows ever so slightly.

"I know that somewhere in this village is a cache of the Tsar's jewels. I don't want to tell you how I know it exists. I also know that Anna knows where these jewels are. The jewels were given to her mother, Elizabeth. When she died, the knowledge of these jewels was passed onto Anna in some way. Anna wears a hidden pin of enormous wealth designed by Fabergé which is proof enough for me."

Loepky's eyes couldn't have gotten bigger. "Jewels?" he breathed.

Mikhail nodded. He could see the man's mind whirling, no doubt already looking for some way to take advantage of all of this.

"Anna?" Disbelief rang in his voice.

Mikhail nodded again.

"Anna wears a piece of jewelry?"

Mikhail nodded. "An extremely valuable piece of jewelry."

"It is forbidden," he said, suddenly assuming an aura of holiness again.

"She wears it only for sentimental reasons on the underside of a collar or whatever, usually hidden from view. I don't think she is even aware of how much that one piece of jewelry is worth."

"And how much is there in this—cache?"

Mikhail smiled. "Enough to exonerate your entire village of taxes for three years, if not more. If you help me find the jewelry, I will see what I can do."

"Who owns this jewelry?"

"Technically the Royal Family owns it. It was given to Elizabeth for safekeeping. I'm sure the arrangement was that in exchange for her trouble she would be gifted with a few pieces of the jewelry. But I don't think Elizabeth cared about the jewelry. I think she just hid it somewhere, because no one seems to know about it. No one can keep secrets—not usually, at least not of this nature—but this woman seems to have. So, she has done an excellent job. I'm not sure Anna even knows. If she does, she too is certainly good at keeping secrets."

Loepky nodded. "We are a close community. For someone to be holding something of this value, and not let anyone know is rare. We usually know everything about each other." He paused. "What if Anna doesn't know?"

"We need to find this cache—whatever it takes. I believe she does know. Somewhere in her subconscious she has got to know. The Royal Family has demanded that we return it now."

"And you are soliciting my help?" Loepky asked.

Mikhail nodded.

"If we find this, our people's tax debt will be forgiven?"

"This deal holds only if you find it. If I find it—you will still be held accountable."

Loepky nodded, his eyes down. "And what is the status now?"

"There is another group, call them what you like: socialists, revolutionaries, rebels, hooligans. There's three men of them that are also looking for the jewelry to fund their movement. They've already abducted and interrogated Nadia."

"Why Nadia?"

"We aren't sure."

"Where is Nadia now?"

"According to Jakob who just arrived home, Nadia is safe at her uncle's, and Aaron is bringing her and Anna home tonight."

"There is a reception tonight—for you."

"I hope to speak to her tonight."

Loepky held out his hand. "I appreciate the offer. I will look into this for you."

Later that evening as Mikhail Kamensky got ready for the evening, he checked his appearance in the mirror. He liked the uniform, though he knew that it would strike a kind of fear, abhorrence in the hearts of these peace-loving Mennonites.

At the reception he would soon find his answers. He would have preferred to use some of Vladimir's tactics, sleuthing from the outside, thieving the information and using brute force to get the cooperation of the people. In hindsight, if he had known that he would have competition, he wouldn't have accepted this official position as a means of getting at the treasure trove. But because he didn't know, his strategy was to try manipulation from the inside. So far he was failing miserably, on all fronts. First of all, not recognizing Anna—he should have known. And then allowing Nadia to be taken from right under his nose.

And now to solicit Loepky, which could be a good idea—or a bad one—depending on how greedy the man was. From the conversation he had assessed Loepky as being very greedy, enough to go after the treasure and steal it. He might take it for himself rather than save the community—something he hadn't considered.

The only good news was that Jakob had come back, a bit winded, his horse almost dead, to let everyone know the girls were safe. Nadia had been roughed up—but had survived. Now Mikhail wondered why Vladimir had allowed Nadia to live. For Vladimir to allow a survivor meant that girl was still of value to him.

The Mayor's garden had been transformed into a outdoor banquet hall. The backyard walks had been raked and swept, the bushes pruned and the sheds painted. Six long tables draped with linens were decorated with peony bouquets and covered with platters of fruit, zwieback, cold meats, jams and assorted cheese.

Mikhail watched with interest. It was nothing like the gala events he had attended at the Winter Palace in St. Petersburg, where over 130,000 people were invited to an evening of heavy partying and brought to the courtyards in more than 4,000 carriages. At those occasions, wine and vodka flowed freely; the jewels and silk dresses of the women were elaborate, and the pomp and ceremony extravagant.

But the politics were always the same. This was a community event and the divisions in the community were obvious. In a population of 2,000, three-quarters had Mennonite roots; the others were of the Adventist, Templer, Catholic, Lutheran or Jewish confession. The Mennonites, or Brethren, because they were dominant, really ignored the others. But all groups were represented here tonight.

The Mayor, who had positioned himself at the front gate, was making a valiant attempt to make everyone feel at home and welcome. His wife Gertrude was working against him, favoring her friends and making the others feel less than welcome. Most of the others, even the Jews, in order to survive, had learned to dress and act Mennonite. They all spoke German and Russian depending on what the situation required.

The women wore black mostly, their hair pulled back in buns. Mikhail could not see one item of jewelry. Even the buttons were black. The entertainment of the evening consisted of endless banter, poking fun at each other—sometimes mercilessly. Often a group of people would spontaneously break out into song, always in a full four-part harmony. And, of course, the food was satisfying, as always.

This was not going to be an easy evening to handle. German was his second language and because of that sometimes he didn't catch the nuances. He was sure they were often smiling at his choice of words behind his back.

Mikhail kept his eyes on the newcomers, making sure that he was introduced to everyone who came. The Mayor stood beside him, doing his best to make the connections. "Now remember, the Neufelds are related to Mrs. Sawatsky, the wife of the wheat farmer, who died last year."

And on and on it went, Mikhail trying to remain attentive to the details of the network of relationships. One never knew when it would become extremely important to know.

The last to arrive was Claus Rempel, a tall man with glasses perched on his nose, an academic-looking man. His wife was tiny by comparison, with thin brown hair and a runny nose. But he did have two lovely daughters, Beth, blonde and Rina had black hair. Everyone noticed them.

Ever since Mikhail had come to the Kuban villages, he had heard constant references to this man.

It was apparent that the village actually knew very little about this man. A hermit by nature, intelligent, eccentric, Rempel had kept a low profile in the community while still maintaining a distant but loyal church member status. Mikhail suspected that gifting a prize-winning stallion to the head pastor, Loepky, helped silence any concerns.

According to the bartender, Slepkov—Rempel was known as a risk taker in the larger community and a shrewd trader in silk and cotton with China. He had accumulated immeasurable wealth but hid it in Swiss banks. He spoke fluent Russian, unlike other Mennonite men his age, and moved easily in the Russian society; he was probably more comfortable there than here in his own community. But he had absolutely no confidence in the Russian market, and thus kept close ties to the Mennonite market.

Mikhail had been waiting to meet this man and was hoping to strike up a conversation with him. But every time he had tried, Rempel, with a warm smile, had excused himself quickly—an elegant, evasive move if ever there was one.

Mikhail watched how the other businessmen quickly congregated around Rempel; but he waved them aside too, making his way to the food. It was the Mennonite food that attracted him to these parties and he would not be distracted. The story was that his wife wasn't much of a cook and when she did cook, she preferred to prepare Russian food, which infuriated him.

Eventually Rempel sat down under a tree with his plate carefully laid out: perishke, cold sausage, pickles, buns and plautz. Others sat down beside him, but he didn't join in their conversations; he was so intent on his food.

Mikhail waited for an opportune time. It came when the man was finally finished eating his third plate of food and chose to sip his coffee—leaning on a fence far removed from the crowd. By this time everyone had left him alone.

Mikhail poured himself a coffee and went to join Rempel—also learning against the fence.

"I hear that you are planning to immigrate to America," Mikhail said softly in Russian. "I hear that you want to catch the next illegal transfer out of here."

Rempel smiled thinly. "You must be a friend of Slepkov."

Mikhail smiled. "I also learned that you gave a horse to Loepky that has now been stolen, which I'm sure will find its way back to your stables."

Rempel's smile broadened. "It has already been returned."

Mikhail paused.

Rempel's eyes narrowed. "And you are Mikhail Kamensky?"

Mikhail nodded.

Rempel sighed. "I didn't want to talk to anyone tonight. I don't want to talk to you either. But I knew you would seek me out. I will not be caught in anything that compromises my beliefs. Contrary to what you believe, I will not betray my people. Vladimir returned the horse, thinking I would help him find the jewels in exchange for his gracious act. Well, I won't. I will return the horse to Loepky at the first opportune moment—probably when both of you have finished your mission and return to St. Petersburg. I have made it very clear to Vladimir to not bother me or interfere with any of my relationships."

Mikhail was silent.

Rempel grew pensive. "I am a good businessman. I do it well. It's what I know. And for that I am handsomely rewarded. However, it does force me to live outside the Mennonite experience. They know I live in another world, a world that they are not sure they understand or could condone. I do things in trade that I am not totally comfortable with; I often live in the gray. But it is what I do best. I do have my code of ethics. I do not participate in cruelty. I know what is dark."

He took a long pause. "Giving my horse to Loepky was not a bribe. My gifts to everyone in this community are not bribes; my donations to missions are not offered out of guilt. This community is my responsibility. My gifts are recognition for the way they look after me and my family.

"In my position I have many opportunities to influence decisions from the outside. I feel it is my duty, my responsibility, to make sure that this community remains alive and safe. I cannot turn my back on them. These are my people and always will be. Some of them are truly wonderful, some of them are evil, and you probably have a good idea who they are already. But that doesn't matter to me; they are my people."

"But you want to immigrate to America."

"What I want and what I do are two very different things. I am open to staying here or leaving, depending on what is needed. America is every businessman's dream. The commerce is vibrant and ethical. Who wouldn't want to go? But unless my farm sells, I won't even contemplate it as a reality"

Mikhail wanted to ask him a lot more questions but stopped. Out of the corner of his eyes, he saw a carriage of four drive onto the yard; he immediately recognized them as

Aaron, Anna, Nadia and a tall young man whom he hadn't met yet—probably Johann. Mikhail stepped back. "Thank you," he murmured, not sure what he was thankful for.

"Watch your step, Mikhail," Rempel warned with a pleasant smile. "I will allow no harm to come to my people—if I can help it."

The minute the carriage stopped in front of the Mayor's home, it was swarmed with people attending the party, asking questions. Someone immediately took Nadia to her room while making arrangements for the doctor to be summoned. Then there was someone who took care of the horses, someone debriefed with Johann, another person with Aaron, and a group of women surrounded Anna, asking her questions, mostly about Nadia.

Anna was conscious that she hadn't thought to change from the green dress she had found in Boris' closet, that she had just spent hours in the carriage facing the wind and sun. They didn't seem to mind. Someone even commented on the dress—the pretty pearl buttons, her hair clip and her new hairstyle. How beautiful she looked, they said. She thought they were just being kind.

Her answer to most of their questions was, "I don't know." Nadia hadn't said much the entire trip, just slept and moaned. She had just made one thing clear that she wanted to be go home—and not stay with her uncle.

Anna had tried to keep her as comfortable as possible, but it had been a hard trip even for herself—someone healthy—let alone for someone already badly injured.

She noticed her stepparents watching her, but neither one of them approached her. This party was a nice reprieve for whatever would come later. She might as well enjoy the lovely evening. And it was lovely. The spring showers had passed. The evening air was moist and warm.

Someone guided her to the buffet table and she chose a few pieces of fruit, some cheese, a dill pickle and a small bun. Lisa, her younger stepsister, came to hug her. In her blended family, Lisa was the only one with whom she had connected. Maria avoided her, pretending to be busy serving. The young people from the church had left quite some time ago to socialize separately; so, she was soon alone watching everyone circulate.

The minute she was alone she felt extremely tired. Perhaps she could slip away into the house and into her room.

"I need to talk to you."

Anna whirled around. It was the one person she had wanted to avoid. Mikhail Kamensky. A firm hand on her elbow led her to a secluded part of the garden, north of the barn. This was where the servants often came for coffee; so, there were a few chairs and a table. She found herself being guided to a chair.

"Sit," he said.

She complied. He sat down opposite her.

"I want a full explanation," he said. "I came here specifically asking to see you, and you run away to a country estate. What was all that about? Pretending you weren't family? Running off before your family got home?"

Anna could tell that he was angry, probably insulted. In hindsight, it now seemed silly, unnecessary and impolite.

But she hesitated. What should she say? "I'm sorry…."

"I think I know why you left. Your parents weren't pleased. Am I right?"

She nodded. "They were concerned…."

"I understand. On the way home, did Nadia tell you anything?"

Anna shook her head. "No, she was really badly beaten. She's in much pain, but she insisted on returning with us. And I'm not sure what that was about."

Mikhail watched her carefully. A slight girl, big brown eyes, dark reddish curly hair. The new hairstyle was becoming. She had an ethereal look of naivete and innocence. Was she as innocent as she appeared? She was hard to read. From what he had gathered, no one knew much about her, except that she had been close to her mother, hated by her stepmother, kind to the servants, a little clumsy, and interested in Russian literature The Russian literature was the only odd quirk that he could find. That too was understandable. She had obviously inherited this interest through her mother and Boris, a Russian nobleman who apparently was just an odd, Russian veteran, shell-shocked by the wars.

Mikhail would have preferred to know more about her but time was of the essence. Any moment Vladimir might make his next move.

"Do you know why I wanted to see you?"

She shook her head.

He would have to brief her quickly so she would understand. "Your Aunt Martha who was shunned from this community, married Viktor, who, worked for the Grand Duke Sergei Alexandrovich, uncle of the Tsar. The Grand Duke was the Governor of Moscow and became an extremely wealthy man. He married a wonderful woman, Elly, the Grand Duchess. The Grand Duke enjoyed investing in jewelry, especially Fabergé, and often the Grand Duke gifted this to his wife, servants and friends. He liked to hide it in unusual places. The short of this is that he gifted some jewelry of considerable value to your uncle and aunt for safekeeping. Viktor could think of only one safe place in all of Russia to hide this jewelry, and that was to give it to Elizabeth, your mother, in a distant Mennonite community for safekeeping. Some of the jewelry was his—but most remained Elly's."

Anna fingered her tiny pin. "That's where this came from?" Her eyes were wide.

Mikhail nodded. "There is much more. That is a lovely, expensive pin—but there are many more pieces of jewelry."

"My mother never breathed a word of this—are you sure this is true?"

"The Grand Duke was assassinated four years ago. The Grand Duchess has been trying to reorganize her life ever since. She is a very generous and religious woman. She has already divested herself of much of her wealth, but she now has a dream to build a convent. She had forgotten entirely about this jewelry until your uncle died a few months ago. On his deathbed he reminded her that she still had some of this jewelry. She has sent me to retrieve what is rightfully hers. You would like the Grand Duchess. You remind me of her. The only reason she wants it now is so that she can help the poor."

Anna's face was ashen. "My mother has died. What if we can't find it?"

"But surely she must have told someone about the jewelry?" Mikhail said softly.

Anna shrugged her shoulders. "I don't know about anyone else, but she didn't tell me."

"Nothing?" Mikhail watched her closely.

"No. She might have told someone else."

"It doesn't appear that way. We think she somehow deposited the secret with you. She must have said something. Your uncle said that you—Anna—had the key to the jewelry."

"He did?"

"Yes."

"I don't—I don't."

"Your mother must have left something behind. She was a person who journalled, I understand."

Anna turned white—something cold and hot spread through her whole body. "You're right—oh, you're right!" Anna stood up. "She left me journals in a box, a tin box—with a key to lock them—and she…." Anna felt anger and tears overtake her. "She did tell me to read them carefully after she was gone. But every time she wanted to talk about things like that, I wouldn't let her. I wasn't ready for her to die."

Anna sat down again, wringing her hands. "I always felt there was something left unsaid but I couldn't read her journals. I couldn't take the pain. So, I kept them safe. But then my stepfather married the Widow Wieler. And she was…." Anna bit her lip. It was hard to say it in words. "She was overbearing. She took control of our lives, which I didn't appreciate, and she knew it. As punishment for my disobedience, she forced me to get the tin box, open it and throw all the journals into the fire. She felt then I would become submissive and a helpful daughter. I was just devastated. I knew I shouldn't have allowed her to burn the diaries. I knew I shouldn't have opened the box. But we are taught to be obedient, and my mother had told me to take care of our father. It was all so confusing."

Anna stopped. "The secret is gone. It is burned. You can go home to St. Petersburg and tell them that they are lost." She unpinned the Fabergé pin. "You can take this back with you. It is the Tsar's." Her lips were trembling, the tears were flowing. "I'm so sorry that I haven't been stronger. I regret every day now that I allowed my stepmother to intimidate me so much. I've just been lost in grief, so lost. I don't know where to turn. I'm so sorry I've lost the secret."

Mikhail put the pin back into her hands. "You don't understand. This an enormous amount of money that we are talking about. It is not only the Tsar who is now interested. The socialist movement feels that the jewels belong to them, so they are also here looking for them."

Anna looked puzzled. "I don't know where they are."

"That isn't good enough. In fact, that is unacceptable. We can't ignore this secret."

"But I don't know where they are." Anna was standing again. "I really don't know. I can't help you. Nor do I care about the jewelry. We Mennonites don't wear jewelry. The only reason I love this pin is because it was from my mother. But I don't want it if it doesn't belong to us. And we don't need the money. We are not interested in money. I have everything I need. I have a dress for every day of the month, plenty to eat, and a warm home. We don't need money that doesn't belong to us."

"None of that matters. You have to lead us to the jewelry."

"I can't." She felt her anger rise. "I can't. I don't know."

"The members of the Socialists movement are the ones who beat Nadia. Remember you switched identities. They overheard Nadia introduce herself to me as Anna—you. That's why they took her. She too probably said she didn't know anything. They didn't believe her. Do you think they will believe you?"

Anna sank into her chair. "They did that to her because—of me?"

Mikhail waited. Anna was shaking like a leaf. Fear grew in her eyes.

"I'm so sorry for Nadia," she gasped, a sob catching in her throat. "How will I ever make it up to her?"

"Nadia is not the one in danger anymore. You are."

"I… I don't… know… I…." She was speechless. Waves of guilt, waves of fear, waves of anger, swept over her again and again. This was all unbelievable. Where had she been—living in some kind of dream world, out of touch with reality? Her mother had wanted to tell her; she had not listened. And yesterday she had run to Boris' leaving Nadia to deal with Mikhail Kamensky, and Nadia had paid dearly.

She took a deep breath. "What can I possibly do? Do you have any ideas?"

Mikhail paused. This was not what he would have wanted. He would have preferred her to deny everything, and thereby signal to him that she knew exactly where the treasure was. Then he could have beaten or scared her into submission and compliance. What if she was right? What if the secret was truly lost forever? They would kill her. He knew that.

He took her hands—sweaty and shaky. "I believe you. But I also believe that your mother told you in many different ways where that jewelry is. I believe she knew that you weren't ready for the knowledge at the time, but I do believe she deposited the secret in you. We now need to take the time to think and remember every word, every action, every walk you took, and every tree she pointed out to you. You need to remember it all. And you need to go to her friends, and talk this through with them. Reminisce together and then you will remember. I am sure."

"Do you really believe that?" She hung onto his hands.

"Yes," he said simply. Frankly he wasn't sure.

"I will sit in my room until I remember."

Mikhail shook his head. "No—I would suggest that you live your life. Tomorrow is Sunday. Do what you have always done. I think it will be as you do things that you will remember."

She nodded. "I will try."

"It's all we can ask."

"I'm tired. I'd like to check on Nadia."

"Don't tell her you know—not yet."

Anna nodded. "I need to be by myself now," she whispered as she melted into the darkness.

Mikhail leaned back and closed his eyes. It had been quite a day. The last two conversations had shaken him to the core of his being. And he wasn't sure why.

"That was quite a conversation you had with Anna."

Mikhail looked up.

"I'm Johann, member of the church council. I have reason to be worried about Anna. I listened in."

Mikhail groaned. "*Blin!*—and what are you going to do about it?"

Johann sat down in the chair that Anna had just vacated. "I understand a lot of what is happening now. Who are you? Who are you that the Duke would trust you to come down all this way and deliver the jewels safely back to the royal family?"

"It's none of your business, *kon 'pedal'nii*," Mikhail said, standing up and leaving.

Chapter ELEVEN

Enjoying his morning solitude, Cornelius Neufeld walked, to his favorite spot on the east side of the barn built on a slight knoll—just high enough to give him a view of his farm and the Kuban villages. The sky to the east was wildly red, glorious, and vivid with sunrise colors.

The morning was his time to look for an inspiration from God. Usually he found something somewhere, even if it was just in the beauty of the rising sun. Sometimes it was in the Bible verses memorized or read, sometimes in a whisper or sometimes in the stirrings of his own soul.

If nothing came, he would begin to recite the words of the Psalms. *I lift up my eyes to the hills. From whence does my help come? My help comes from the Lord, who made heaven and earth. He will not let my foot be moved.*

This morning the poetic words of the Psalm moved him. *He who keeps you will not slumber… the Lord is your shade on your right hand… The Lord will keep you from all evil; he will keep your life.*

He particularly liked the benediction. *The Lord will keep your going out and your coming in from this time forth and forevermore.*

It was Sunday morning, and it was on these holy days that he often felt the entire weight of the community come to rest on his prayer-weary shoulders. He would never admit it to anyone, certainly not boast of it, but sometimes he felt that he was cursed or blessed with knowing and feeling too much.

Without ever really talking to the people, he seemed to know just by watching from his perch on the hill what was happening in their lives. The insights came from the little things like the lights turning on too early; an early light in a child's room might mean sickness or a nightmare. A light on late at night could mean a tired, over-worked parent, with financial troubles. A man chopping wood with too much vigor was as telling as a man chopping without vigor. It was the little things like someone walking to a house they shouldn't be walking to. Sometimes it was someone praying, reading by a light in their parlor window; sometimes it was in the good that they did; sometimes it was in the evil. But he had learned long ago his was not to judge. His was to love. His was to try and see it all through God's eyes. His was to pray.

Sometimes it was hard not to judge. From his perch he could see Loepky's farm. More and more it was becoming apparent that the man was up to something. The man had moved into their community about five years ago, a rather poor farmer. It was not unusual for lead pastors to be poor farmers. It was the price they paid for putting so much of their energy and time into the church—an expected sacrifice of being a leader in a Mennonite community. Neufeld was fortunate; he had many sons who had picked up the slack at this farm, freeing him to tend to the flock. The problem was that Loepky seemed to resent being poor. He wanted it all, and he was getting all. He was growing richer, and the sources of that wealth weren't always clear. It was obvious that Loepky wanted to be the most powerful man in the community, not for any particular reason, but that he loved the feeling of being powerful. It was something that Neufeld had seen happen to many of their leaders. The end was never good. Usually both the leader and the church suffered much in the process. Neufeld wanted to warn the members of the church, but he couldn't. Because Loepky had usurped Neufeld's position as lead pastor, the community would see his warnings as sour grapes. Yet Neufeld truly didn't want the position. The people only saw the glory of the position; they didn't see the responsibility. As the years went by, he no longer saw the glory, only the responsibility, and the responsibility was becoming increasingly heavy with age. He longed for the day when he would be free of all of it.

Neufeld leaned forward, putting his head in his hands to pray for his wife, his children, for Johann, and then for everyone in the community. He let the tears flow down his cheeks unchecked—such was his burden for them.

When he raised his head, he saw a rider wearing a white shirt billowing behind him, veering to the west, riding close along the fence. It was Aaron Franz obviously hoping to get home before anyone noticed him missing. The boy liked the wild nightlife. He was being driven by something.

Anna too was not doing well. Yesterday at the Mayor's reception, he had seen Mikhail watching Anna. He had seen Johann watching Anna. He had seen Loepky's eyes on Anna. All of their expressions were unreadable.

As for Johann, he could understand his interest—Anna was an attractive, lovely available, young woman. What interested the other two wasn't as clear—and that worried him.

In the fog of half sleep, Anna woke gasping for air. In her dreams, she had been searching all night, running in a watery garden with thousands of distant voices calling out to her; inky black shapes wavered in the gloom; specters floated in the deep; a nightmare of ghastly images held out their arms to her. She was running away from their painful, lonely faces until she noticed that her mother was with them, one of them—thin, sad and wavering in the shadows. Her mother had called out to her, moaning, and crying with outstretched arms that couldn't reach across the dark mist. Anna had turned and, stretching out her own arms, began to run frantically towards her mother. But a strong, cold current held her back.

Struggling with her blankets, she awoke with the dream still clinging to her. The sight of her mother had brought back devastating grief. Her head swirled in pain. She had to concentrate just to breathe, just to sit up in her bed. Slowly she became aware that someone else was in the room.

Nadia was sitting quietly at the window still in her nightgown, the bandages obscuring most of her face. "Nightmare?"

Anna brushed the hair from her face. "Yes." She held her breath to stop her pounding heart.

"I've been having nightmares too."

Anna felt waves of remorse descend on her. "I'm so sorry, Nadia, about the beating. I had no idea. I just thought it was a case of mistaken identity."

"I'm glad it was me, not you."

Anna swung her legs off the bed. "You can't say that. They almost killed you. And you're still in pain. I can tell by the way you sit."

"Do you know what they are after?" Nadia asked.

"Yes, Mikhail told me everything."

Nadia sat quietly. "And they told me everything."

Anna sighed—everything was out—and apparently Nadia was in the middle of it. "Nadia, except for the pin my mother gave me before she died, I know nothing about the jewelry"

"They will not stop till they find it," Nadia murmured.

"I know. Mikhail warned me of that. But I can't remember anything."

"You have to."

"I can't conjure up a memory I don't have. I don't know."

"They won't stop."

"They will have to once they realize I simply don't know. If my mother did leave me a clue to where this cache of jewelry is hidden, it was burnt in the journals."

Nadia's eyes grew wide. "Those journals…," she said slowly, remembering the dreadful scene. Anna was screaming as if she was being ripped asunder, then she changed turning into stone—a pure white stone, regal in her pain— as Widow Wieler forced her in front of the fire to burn all those pages.

"Yes, it was probably in those journals. And I never read them."

"Never read them?"

"No, I couldn't open them after my mother died. It was too painful. I never read them."

Nadia's dark eyes were moist. "They won't believe that."

Anna was on her feet. "They have to believe that those jewels are lost. We can't very well comb every inch of this community, dig up every foot of it! The jewels are gone. I will give them my brooch. That is all I have."

"They won't be satisfied until all the jewels are in their hands."

"What do you want me to do?" Anna wailed.

"Try."

"Try? What does that mean?"

"I don't know. It was your cat that killed the swallow. You have to find those precious jewels or we are all dead." With that, Nadia struggled to her feet, wincing painfully as she straightened.

"I can't, Nadia." Anna followed Nadia as she slowly, painfully, made her way down the hall. "I can't."

Nadia did not answer. She did not look back as she gingerly made her way down the stairs.

For some time, she sat at the edge of her bed staring at her reflection in the tiny wood-framed mirror on her dresser. Hot rage boiled inside her. She could not do it. Whatever they expected, she just couldn't do it. Why hadn't she listened to her mother more attentively? Why hadn't she read the diaries?

They wanted her to remember! She put her head in her hands. The only thing she could remember was one of their final conversations. It had been snowing outside. Her mother had been bundled in layers and layers of blankets; yet she still shivered under them.

"You need to read the diaries, Anna," her mother had said. "I've written something important for you in them."

Anna had nodded.

"Anna, you must remain strong. You must be there for your father. He will be lost for a while."

The memory of those words was particularly painful. Who would have thought that the Mayor would marry within the year to the dreadful Widow Wieler?

Her mother had then given her a handkerchief for the tears that flowed down her cheeks. "Don't fret, Anna. It isn't over. It is only goodbye for a short time." But, here on earth, a year could seem like an eternity.

Then her mother had given her advice.... Anna tried to remember. It was all so vague now. She could remember her mother turning to the window... gazing intently out of the window, and then she heard the voice again. "If you are ever in doubt of anything, go and talk to the ministers of the church.

Cornelius Neufeld is the man I have relied on for spiritual counsel—or any counsel for that matter. He is a wise man." Anna was disappointed; the memory of the advice contained nothing about the jewels. But it was all she had.

Anna went to her closet and took out a black silk blouse that was pleated smartly down the front, and a heavy brocaded black skirt that fit snugly around her waist and hips flowing into a full-length skirt.

She had made up her mind. She would go to church as she always did on Sunday mornings, and then later she would go and see Cornelius Neufeld as her mother had suggested. It was the best and only thing she could do.

She wrapped her hair up into a loose bun and pulled tendrils from it to frame her face. Yesterday, everyone seemed to comment on this new hairstyle. A braided bun no longer seemed appropriate. Something had changed in her. Before she would have worried about the reaction of Widow Wieler to any change in her appearance—now it didn't matter. Anna had an overpowering agenda, which made most everything else appear secondary.

The family was waiting for her in the kitchen. Mikhail Kamensky was sitting at the kitchen table, sipping coffee. He was watching her. He had only one question. "Anything yet?"

She shook her head. "I'm going to church." There was no need for small talk.

He nodded. "And I'm going to ride the countryside. I might be able to talk sense into the thieves."

She nodded. "When will you be back?"

"Probably late evening."

Anna noticed that both Gertrude and the Mayor were watching them closely. It was obvious that Mikhail had told them everything. It was also obvious that something had changed in them as well. They were watching her as if she too were a guest in their house.

The church, built simply of plain white clapboard, was already filling when she arrived. Knots and clusters of people moved in together, the men using the door on the right, the women the one on the left.

The inside of the building was furnished with long benches of roughly hewn wood, stretching from wall to wall with one aisle down the middle. Again, the men sat on the right, the women on the left. The only decoration was a simple cross hanging on the front whitewashed wall made of the same wood as the benches. On a raised platform in front there was no altar but a pulpit, bulky and new, the top draped with a red cloth, and on that a large Bible. To the side were a few more benches for the choir. At the very back, almost hidden, there was also a little piano with a tiny mirror for the pianist to watch the choir director.

Anna noticed that people stopped whispering when she walked by. She wondered how many in the community knew about the jewels. Were they talking about Nadia, the beating, the abduction, the visit to Boris' for the books? There was certainly a lot to talk about.

Everyone knew his or her place. Anna knew hers was next to the window. The most striking features of the building were the huge, multi-paned windows built low for the parishioners to see outside. It was the only extravagance. Anna sat near the back. With her mother, she had chosen this place a long time ago as a child so she could always look outside the window and dream about whatever she wanted to.

It was amazing how by simply turning her head and surveying the gathering congregation, she knew instantly who was missing, who was talking to whom, and who was sitting with whom. Every change was noticeable.

Gazing around she noticed when Johann walked through the door. People paused to watch him pass. She could read their minds. He was an important newcomer. His father had been a well-known pastor in the mother colonies; he was already a wealthy farmer, and had become known for his inventiveness. They had immediately placed him on the church council to honor his position. It was almost as if they were bowing to him already. It disgusted her. These people prided themselves on thinking everyone was equal, the priesthood of all believers; yet there was a status—a painful status that ignored the less fortunate.

Johann paused deliberately at the door, slowly appraising the room, his eyes finding hers. He nodded in recognition with an expression that seemed almost as if he was surprised to see her in church. She knew what he was thinking—he was surprised that someone as vile as her, who read Russian literature, would come to church. It seemed as if she was determined to remain part of the church until she was officially shunned.

Then he slowly and deliberately walked to the front to sit with the other church council members. He was by far the youngest of all the men.

The pastor George Loepky stood behind the pulpit, opened the large pulpit Bible and began to read. He was tall, nearly six two, an imposing man both straight and trim. Past fifty, his hair remained thick, and he allowed himself the vanity of wearing it brushed back like a flowing white mane. He sported a neat beard and moustache that surrounded his rather thin mouth.

With his dramatic, eloquent style of delivery, the people said that they didn't sleep through his sermons. How could one? Anna listlessly looked out the window to watch a few latecomers unhitching their horses in the adjoining field that served as a parking space for the horses and carriages.

She couldn't sleep through his sermons either, but it wasn't because she found him riveting. On the contrary, it was because she found his style grating, his delivery pompous and his constant themes of sin, damnation and pressure to go out and save the lost Russian souls hollow. No one cared for the Russian souls in this church, not really. The government in fact had forbidden them to proselytize; yet it was the same thing every Sunday morning. His sermons were designed to be guilt-inducing sermons that convicted mercilessly, and for what reason? No one did anything differently throughout the week. It was almost as if the congregation had become accustomed to a certain amount of administered pain on Sunday so that their guilt would be assuaged for the week. Anna distracted herself by allowing her eyes to drift outside, watching the clouds, watching the restless horses, and watching the birds as she tried to remember something about her mother.

"To read anything other than God's word is sin. To read a best-selling Russian novel is a sin," Loepky declared.

Anna looked up. Loepky's piercing eyes were focused on her. In spite of herself, she felt the blood rush to her cheeks and there was nothing she could do to bring down the color. Then with the spotlight firmly fixed on her, he went on to use his enormous skill and eloquence to damn all worldly influence; he specifically mentioned the evil influence of Russian stories, myths and culture. By the end of his sermon, she felt like a red flare, her hair standing on end, her perspiring skin glistening and reflecting her discomfort. To leave would have called even more attention to herself—besides she was hemmed in on all sides.

She was tremendously relieved when the choir got up to sing their one song from the Liederperlen song book, accompanied beautifully by her own dear brother, Aaron, who looked a little out of sorts this morning, his hair standing on end, his suit jacket rumpled, and a dirty handkerchief hanging out of his back pocket. But at least he played marvelously.

And then it was Cornelius Neufeld's turn to speak. The contrast between the two speakers was immediate. Neufeld was bald, with a shiny dome-like head, red cheeks, red nose, and huge watery blue eyes. It seemed as if he was always on the verge of tears, ready to cry for them all. And he was old. He had a much quieter demeanor, often quoting scripture directly from the Bible. His messages were of God's love, mercy and grace.

But today it was hard to concentrate even on this sermon. All she could think of was the jewels. Was it really as critical as everyone thought? Would the revolutionaries really not listen to any kind of reasoning? What if they killed her? What if they killed Nadia? Her heart began to race. What if they beat her, as they had beaten Nadia? She wasn't as strong as Nadia....

In his very quiet way, Neufeld began to penetrate her consciousness. "Anyone who loses his life... will find it, Jesus says, reminding us that love is purified in pain."

His voice was low, smooth and comforting. "Prayer is far from sweet and easy. But prayer is the expression of our greatest love. Remaining in prayer does not keep pain away from us. Instead, it makes us suffer more since our love for God is a love for a suffering God and our entering into God's intimacy is an entering into the intimacy where all of human suffering is embraced in divine compassion."

Someone was breathing heavily behind her, falling asleep. She glanced behind her. Sure, enough it was Hildebrand who always slept in church but then in her glance she noticed the uniform in the back row. How long had Mikhail been listening? She hadn't noticed him before. Wasn't he suppose to be out there gathering intelligence? Maybe this was one of his stops? Maybe he would learn more than he expected to? Glad he was hearing Neufeld and not Loepky....

Anna turned back to listen to Neufeld with a new set of ears. He was now leaning on the pulpit—tears were rolling down his cheeks.

"To the degree that our prayer has become the prayer of our heart we will love more and suffer more. We will see more light and more darkness, more grace and more sin, more of God and more of humanity. To the degree that we have descended into our hearts and reached out to God from there, solitude can speak to solitude, deep to deep and heart to heart. It is there where love and pain are found together."

Her heart stopped racing. She could feel her color recede. She didn't understand the depth from which he was speaking, but it was enough to know that he was there, he understood, and that he would help her understand some day. For now, she had heard that God was in her pain. God was not condemning her.

When they were finally singing the last hymn and Loepky gave the closing benediction, she turned to check on Mikhail—he had left. So, she took a moment to just sit in silence—reluctant to leave. She hadn't uncovered any memories of her mother here in church, at least none that would act as a clue to the whereabouts of the jewels, but she had been reminded of God.

When the building was almost empty, she got up.

"I need to speak to you," she whispered to Neufeld as she greeted him at the door.

"Mid-afternoon?"

She nodded.

Walking home from church, alone, quickly to avoid questions, she had been lost in thought till she turned the corner where the whole house came into view. Something about the house was amiss.

She paused. Any other time she wouldn't have even noticed but with all that was happening she was becoming more aware of the tiniest warnings of harm. She allowed her eyes to examine the house, the barn where Nadia was sleeping and then back to the house. And then she saw it. Her window was broken, her curtain torn.

She began to run. Once inside the house, she bolted down the hall that connected the house to the barn, and into Nadia's room. Her room was dark. Anna could make out a form, curled up in a blanket, sleeping. She was breathing evenly and deeply.

Anna backed out of the room, and ran up the stairs to her own room. She could feel her hair disengaging, falling over face. The door was hanging by its hinges. Holding her breath, she peered inside.

The curtains were shredded, her bed torn apart, the mattress stabbed a hundred times. The clothes from her closet had been thrown into the middle of the floor and stomped on with heavy, muddy boots. Most of the dresses had also been deliberately slashed. The drawers of her dresser had been emptied—the contents either torn, muddied or destroyed in some way. Her window had been broken. And on the walls, in heavy red paint was the one word, "Murder."

Her entire room had been trashed. Anna dragged her hands through her hair. It couldn't get much worse than this. And then she noticed that on top of her once neatly organized dresser was the picture of her mother. It had been ripped in two. Over the roaring in her head, she could hear her own low moan as she reached for it—holding it together as if that would somehow mend it. She had so little left of her mother....

She backed out of the room. Her brother was behind her. "I'm so sorry," he whispered in a hollow voice. "I'm so sorry. So sorry."

"No," she made a fist with her hands, digging her nails into her palms until the pain cut through the shock. "They can't do this to me. They can't frighten me like this."

But it was already done. Even her stepmother seemed sympathetic, her stepfather grim, and the rest of the family watched her, wide-eyed and nervous.

"This is not good," Gertrude said over and over again. "They have come into our house. What will they do next? They have no shame. They have no fear."

Maria, her older stepsister, guided her down the stairs to the garden table underneath the grape arbor. "We will fix your room. You just stay here."

Lisa, her younger stepsister, only ten years old, brought her a plate of roast beef and tomatoes, then sat with her. She noticed Jakob and Aaron both watching her from afar, as if they were ready to protect her, but too frightened to enter into her grief.

She sat there in shock, rocking in her pain, as one by one they came to her offering her condolences. Grief swarmed over her, stinging like wasps.

As time passed, Maria came off and on to tell her that she had salvaged the brown dress—maybe the blue one, definitely the mauve one—but the yellow and the white were ruined. She was full of good news one time, and bad news the next.

"At least we don't own much," she said finally. "Compared to our Rempel friends we have very little. They had no jewels to steal…."

At that point, Anna opened her mouth to say something, but the would-be words trailed away, no sound, just her harsh gasps, as she tried to remain calm. But then dissolved into tears.

It felt good to cry. It was the only good feeling left.

Chapter TWELVE

"Welcome to my office," Neufeld chuckled, inviting her to sit down in the chair opposite him. "I was expecting you earlier…."

She smiled wanly, gratefully taking the chair, still trying to calm her ragged breath.

"Interesting place you have," she said, looking around the room. The space was filled with shelves of books, old chairs, and tables hosting various creative projects. One particular station was notably cluttered with books.

This was Cornelius Neufeld's office—a typical *Aeltester.*

Then she noticed Johann sitting in the corner.

She turned to Neufeld. "I was hoping to talk to you in private," she whispered. She couldn't concentrate with Johann around. It was going to be hard enough to keep her composure that she was fitting so hard to maintain. "I think it is important to keep this…."

"Is your visit about the jewels?" Neufeld interrupted her.

Anna was shocked. "Yes—how did you know?"

"Johann has just been filling me in with all the details."

"But how does he know?" she asked, giving him a scathing look.

Nonplussed, Johann came over and sat down next to her. "I heard Mikhail talking to you yesterday."

She was horrified. "You eavesdropped?"

"It was more than idle curiosity, Anna. I saw Mikhail forcing you to go with him to an isolated part of the yard. After what I had seen and heard all day, I was concerned.

She glared at him. "You heard it all?"

He nodded. "I thought you might need protection."

"Protection?" She was disgusted. Nadia had needed protection and there was no one there for her. Mikhail was a safe person to be with!

Neufeld leaned forward. "Anna, Johann is already involved and he has been helpful. Will you allow him to be part of this conversation?"

She hesitated, then nodded. "I don't know where to begin."

"Pretend I know nothing, and tell me everything."

Neither of them knew what they were asking of her. All her life she had wanted to avoid being noticed by the church council, and now they were asking her to bare her soul. Yet she was desperate.

It took almost an hour to tell him everything because of his gentle but probing questions.

"Now do you see why I am afraid? They will stop at nothing to find these jewels, I am told, and I don't think I can help them. I'm not sure they'll believe me. They ransacked my room this morning when we were all in church." Anna drew in a breath. Then she described in vivid detail how they had desecrated her room. "I am becoming desperate" she said softly.

For a long moment, the men sat stunned. "It is truly unfortunate that Gertrude burnt those diaries," Neufeld said finally, leaning back, his hand stroking his stubby goatee.

Then Neufeld leaned forward. "I don't believe that the clues are gone, Anna. I don't believe you have exhausted all the possibilities."

"Did my mother tell you anything?"

"No. We were good friends but we talked mainly about family. She often told me how concerned she was for her children. I will examine my memories, but I think it is more important that we examine yours."

Johann nodded. "Think hard, Anna. Is there anything?"

Anna leaned back, her head against the old chair, eyes closed, thinking, shaking her head. "I have been over everything."

"Do you have anything that belongs to your mother that you haven't told us about?"

Johann watched her carefully. Almost lost in the huge chair, her face pale with fear, and her hair an absolute frizzy mess, she looked vulnerable, almost angelic.

Anna opened her eyes. "I do have a worn Bible and an old novel that belonged to my mother. But neither one of them has a note or anything in them. I've read both since she died, and neither of them hold anything of interest other than what they mean to me."

"Where are these?"

"In a very special hiding place where I knew Widow Wieler wouldn't look. But I really don't think they are of importance."

"Let us be the judge of that. Why don't you get them, or anything else that you remember was your mother's."

"Are you sure?"

Neufeld and Johann nodded.

Anna stood up slowly. "Can this wait until the morning? It's getting dark and I'm exhausted."

Neufeld shook his head. "This time we need to insist. We haven't much time."

Ana looked weary. "All right."

"Take Johann with you and come back here," Neufeld added.

"I can go by myself. I don't need anyone," she said curtly.

Neufeld took her hands. "Anna, humor me."

"Are you sure he wants to do this with his precious time?" she asked sarcastically.

"Why do you doubt?"

Anna rolled her eyes. "I don't think he believes I am a member in good standing. I read Russian literature like my mother did."

Neufeld glanced over her shoulder to study Johann's expression. His face was unreadable. His eyes were dark under heavy lids, and shadowed by sweeping black brows. Johann remained a brooding presence. "Johann, is that right?"

Johann cleared his throat. "From what I've seen, Nadia beaten and all, I have grave concerns that Anna is in serious danger. What I think of her interests doesn't matter at the moment."

Neufeld smiled into Anna's eyes. "Humor me. Take him with you."

"I guess I have no choice," Anna said walking to the door.

Neufeld followed her. "Nothing else matters until those jewels are found."

At the door Neufeld briefly put his arm around her, feeling her tremble. He wished he could take away her fear. But he also knew that this was her time to face her fears. "Anna, you need to know that when you were coming home from Boris', Johann tells me that there was someone following you. He is convinced that it was Nadia's abductors. Someone is probably watching us this very moment."

"Do you really think so?" she whispered hoarsely, her eyes scanning the edges of the yard.

"Yes," Neufeld said patting her arm. "At this point I wouldn't entrust you to even our Russian guards. Do not do anything without Johann." He turned to Johann. "Take two horses, get the Bible and novel, and bring them back here so we can start to work on them. Take the good horses… Joshua and Moses. One never knows."

"Are you sure?"

Neufeld nodded.

Anna couldn't help but admire the meticulous barn, and the well-groomed horses as she walked down the middle corridor of the barn. Neufeld's horses weren't Oldenburgers from Germany, the horse of choice in the Kuban villages; his were the popular Don, a Russian breed favored by the Cossacks.

She had often heard Neufeld say that he preferred power to beauty, endurance over speed. He didn't break his horses like the others; he coaxed them, talked to them, listened to them, treated them well, and for that they would do anything he wanted. Because of that they were also known in the broader community as being exceptionally well trained.

"Do you prefer to take a buggy or to ride a horse?" Johann asked.

Anna hadn't ridden since her mother died. At first it was because she didn't care to go out—there was no place to go. Then, when Widow Wieler had come into their home, it had been forbidden. Women didn't ride horses. They only rode in carriages.

"I want to ride a horse," Anna said. "And Molly here will do just fine."

Johann shook his head as he continued down the center of the barn, finally coming to two huge chestnuts that were rested and well fed. Unhitching them, he walked them out of the barn to the tack room.

"Are you sure?" Anna asked, following him. "I would hate to be responsible for them if something went wrong."

Johann only smiled. "Neufeld said to take the best. These are the best."

In no time they had saddled the two, and were riding back to Anna's house. The horses trotted easily down the village street. It had been a long time since she had ridden, and she loved the feel of the horse moving easily, powerful and responsive to the tiniest message of her hands. She had chosen to ride sidesaddle, and hated the awkwardness of it. She would have much preferred to ride astride, and feel more in control of the massive horse but one didn't do that in public.

When they reached the house, Anna reined in her horse and slid off her mount. "This shouldn't take too long. You can wait outside if you like."

"No," Johann said, dismounting from his horse and tying both horses to a hitching post, and following her. "I was told to protect you, and from what I've seen, I intend to keep you in my sight at all times."

She rolled her eyes with disgust. Even though she was very aware that she was being targeted, she still resented the patronizing attitude he was taking.

He followed her into the barn. "Is this where you keep your Bible and novel? In a barn?" he asked, surprised.

Suddenly she was embarrassed that she had to hide her most precious possessions up in the furthest corner of a dusty, cobwebbed hay loft so that her stepmother wouldn't find them—nor those looking for jewels. "You can wait down here," she said.

He shook his head.

She shrugged her shoulders, and started up the narrow stairs leading to the loft. At the top of the stairs, she moved some old boxes and pulled out a tin box.

"This is it," she said, holding it out for him to see—the color flooding into her cheeks. She was very aware of how pathetic she must look. This was all that was left of her personal life—an old, battered tin box full of two worn books that she couldn't even read or keep in her room.

He sensed her humiliation. He was seeing her differently now than the first time he had met her at Boris' house. There she had been part of Boris' world, eccentric, wild, and mysterious. At the church, she had been one of the women, on the other side of the church, submissive, obedient and serene. At Neufeld's she had been frightened, confused and vulnerable; now she was shy, reticent, and apologetic.

He took the Bible carefully from the box, and paged through it. It was an old book, well used and marked. He flipped to the back pages; there were lists of references, words, and a few scribbled drawings. This was promising. Any one of these writings could be a clue. He noticed the words, "Hidden in a box, in the church" written in elegant handwriting—that was promising. Since it was underlined, it was probably a hint as to what they were looking for. "I think we need to get this back to Neufeld as fast as we can. With his knowledge of the Bible and the community, I think he can help us."

She took it from him, scanning the pages. "The notes look different now. Before, these handwritten notes were just sentimental nothings."

He nodded.

Closing the book carefully, she put the books back into the tin box.

He took the box from her and put it into his knapsack then stepped outside.

"I should check on Nadia." Anna hesitated at the door.

Johann shook his head. "No time. You'll be back soon. We need to do this first."

Chapter THIRTEEN

They needed to get back to Neufeld.

Johann was suddenly feeling edgy again. The sky was changing. The day, which had started as cloudless, was now graying. But it was more than that. His spine prickled. Someone was watching them.

Anna scanned the sky too. She picked up a cloak and offered him one too.

He helped Anna onto her horse. "Here, you hang onto the knapsack. We'll attach it to your saddle." He took his time to attach it well. Mounting his own horse, he led the way down the driveway.

Suddenly he heard the sound of horses. He turned in time to see three riders emerge from behind the barn on their horses in full gallop. They had been hiding there, watching. They had probably seen the package, and noticed the care he had taken to attach it. They knew! And, in turn, he knew exactly what they had in mind.

"Anna," he shouted, "we need to make a run for it."

She nodded; she had seen them too. She snapped the reins and her large horse, charged ahead. In seconds they were in full gallop. The horses, sensing the chase, needed no encouragement.

At first Johann let Anna take the lead, wanting to stay between her and the pursuers. Anna didn't turn or look back. She was bent on her task, her dark cloaked form hunched forward over the horse as it ran.

The problem was that they needed to turn right to get back to Neufeld's but the three pursuers were angling in on the right side, anticipating their turn. The only option was to surprise them. He pushed his horse even harder till he was racing next to Anna and headed her off to the left. Her eyes were saucers of fear as she threw him a puzzled look.

He pulled in front of her. "Follow me," he said.

The only chance they had was to keep running until they had outdistanced their pursuers. But their options were minimal. They were already at the edge of the village, fast approaching a major fork in the road. Once choice was to take the road that followed the river to Stavropol, the other was to take the road along the railway tracks that would take them to Rostov.

Images of Nadia's face after the beating kept flashing through Johann's mind. He couldn't bear to think of Anna suffering through anything like that. They just had to get away safely, at any cost. Probably the road along the railway tracks that would take them to Rostov.

The trick had worked; the pursuers had slowed down to make the right-hand turn, and in so doing had fallen behind significantly.

Johann did not let up the pace.

Every once in a while, he turned to see how Anna was doing. Somewhere along the way she had abandoned any pretense of riding sidesaddle daintily. She had swung her leg over and was riding astride, her skirt hiked to her thighs, her cloak billowing behind her. There was a lot of leg showing, but he couldn't allow himself to notice.

She gave him a thin-lipped, faint, reassuring smile to let him know that she was all right. But her eyes remained saucers of fear.

The road narrowed. They hung on as their horses continued to pound down on the dirt road, kicking up clumps of dirt. It was getting darker now. The mist had turned into rain. Heavy raindrops pelted Johann's face. Each one, a small cold prick which, heated and mingled with sweat, ran down his neck. He suspected Anna was just as uncomfortable.

The darkness—the threat of rain might work in their favor—the thieves that had already fallen behind seemed to be slowing down. When the way was wide enough, Johann fell back to ride beside Anna and reined in his horse till he was trotting. Anna did the same.

"I think they've fallen back." He turned around, listening. He couldn't hear anything. "I think they might be thinking that we will turn around because of the rain—and the dark. They're probably waiting for us to come back."

She nodded. Some of her hair was stuck sideways across her face. "This is the way to Boris'," she said. "Should we go there?"

He shrugged. "What do you think?"

Anna flicked the hair from her face. "It's a long way."

"Do we have a choice?"

She shook her head.

"Are you up to it?"

"I don't want to go back." Her teeth were chattering. Chattering teeth? That in itself would have been a good enough reason to turn back. She was in shock, trembling. They weren't prepared for this journey. The cloaks weren't going to be warm enough. They had no resources. What if they got lost? Then she thought of the alternative.

"I'm not going back," she said with conviction. It was as if she was reading his mind as well.

"Besides Boris has a gun. He will protect us once we get there."

That was the irony of their situation—two Mennonites, peace-loving, fleeing into the rainy night, heading out to the only place they felt safe, to a mad man with a gun. But it wasn't the time to discuss values and beliefs. Both weren't about to turn back into the waiting ambush.

Johann took the lead again. They continued down the dismal road, slower now watching the woods as they went. Tree trunks stood like black pillars in the murky darkness.

The road was beginning to traverse a hillside, and he could see dark rocks rising up to their left.

Eventually, as it got too dark to see, he let his horse pick its own way in the gathering night, wondering how much longer this ride would take. The night was bringing life to the woods, strange calls and scraping noises. His horse whinnied at things unseen. He patted his horse's neck reassuringly.

Following behind, Anna concentrated on keeping her horse close to Johann's. Her heart was pounding fiercely, occasionally lurching when she heard a new, unfamiliar sound. She was replacing one fear with another. Perhaps they weren't being pursued but the woods at night was another worry. There were wolves out here; there were other thieves, other threats just as serious.

Her horse stopped when Johann's horse stopped.

She pulled up beside Johann. "What?" she asked softly.

"Do you know where we are?"

"We're still on the road to Boris'."

"How far are we from Boris' farm?"

"I don't know that." She paused. "We're taking a long way around. I have rarely traveled this road. I can hardly find my way there in the daylight. Now that it's dark…." Her voice was breathless, nervous.

There was a hoot nearby. The horses stamped about skittishly.

The road had become muddy, slick and slimy. The horses were sliding.

"I think we should walk them." Johann slid off his horse.

Anna followed suit. She had worn the wrong shoes for this uneven road.

They walked in silence, afraid to even whisper in the dark, close to each other, sharing the same troubled thoughts without expressing them. They had to watch their step. Slipping and sliding she trudged on, wrapping her cloak tightly around herself.

The horses were as nervous as they were. Then Anna stumbled on a branch that had fallen into the mud tried to recover, slipped and almost fell.

Johann caught her, and held her.

The horses stopped. Everything stopped.

She could feel his arms tighten, bringing their bodies closer. Feeling his warmth, she could not resist moving closer—their bodies molding together as if they fit.

She looked up just as he was looking down at her. He bent down as she was reaching….

Even in the dark their lips found each other—somehow knowing the unknown. Needing mutual comfort and warmth their lips locked in a moment of bliss, moving, sharing something moist and sensual. She felt her knees turn to water—she was losing herself—dangerously.

She pulled back…. "No…." she whispered breaking the moment. "We mustn't." His arms loosened but still held her until she found her feet again.

"No, we mustn't." Then paused. "But are you alright? Can we continue?"

He was a voice in the dark, a comforting arm around her waist.

She was exhausted. "Yes," she said meekly.

His hand had slipped down to find her hand. His touch was reassuring and helpful, as it was meant to be. It was also large, warm, and a bit rough from outside work. She noticed that her hand fit into his perfectly. Any other time, she would have considered it imprudent, as a single woman, to be walking hand-in-hand with a young man, alone, in the dark and unchaperoned.

But—she needed that hand in the dark. She had needed that kiss.

They continued to walk in silence. She found herself fighting back the tears. She was a mess. She wasn't used to being interrogated, chased, riding horse, slipping in the mud, being kissed and then continuing to walk and walk. She wasn't sure how much longer she could walk. Her legs were trembling, her teeth chattering, and her mind was numb with fear.

Suddenly he stopped. "I think I hear something."

She listened. "It's a train."

"This time of night?"

"They travel at all times."

"It sounds close."

"That means we are almost there. The train and road run parallel for almost an entire verst."

They stopped to watch the train approach, a huge beam of light, winding its way along the river's edge, coming closer, closer and then veering off, leaving them standing in the darkness. It had made them feel strangely safer, not so alone in the dark woods. In the fleeting light, Anna looked around to get her bearings.

“Yes—I know where we are now. There’s an intersection up ahead. And then we turn to the right.”

They continued walking. The rain had stopped but the mist clung to them, forcing them to the edge of the road onto the wild grasses. Water dripped from the leaves as they passed under the trees.

Finally, when they least expected it, the clouds broke and they saw the moon, only a sliver but enough to shed a remarkable amount of silver light.

“I think we can ride again,” Johann said, noticing that the dirt road was more overgrown with grass and would presumably be less slippery.

Johann could tell that Anna was more tired than she wanted to let on as he helped her remount.

At least the tension between them had eased, thought Anna as she followed his silhouette through the trees. They rode in silence for another endless stretch. Her wariness and fear had dulled. All her efforts now were to stay on her horse that was automatically following the lead horse, and to keep warm somehow. The breeze was cool, and she felt chilled to the bone. Her horse nearly bumped into his, when Johann stopped suddenly.

“Shh,” he warned Anna. He listened. He heard a soft scraping sound again, slightly ahead of him. The sound was too deliberate, too human. He guided his horse onto a path beside the road, urging the horse to move more quickly. He was grateful for the moonlight that was making it possible to choose his way more deliberately. Was there something on the road ahead of them?

Then he saw the shadows lounging against the trees. There were faint outlines of horses tied to trees. Had the three riders had taken the shorter and faster route along the river?

"Anna," he whispered, waving to the shadows. She saw and nodded. Then he spurred his horse into a full gallop.

The shadows heard them coming. There was a yell, some scrambling, and then the shadows leapt onto their horses. But by this time, Johann and Anna had already moved past them.

Johann turned to see if Anna was keeping up with him. She was hunched down on her horse, molding herself to its moving body. When he saw an opening, he veered from the path onto the open road again, still urging the horse to run.

Johann let Anna take the lead, she knew the way to Boris' place better than he did. She would know when to turn.

The sound of pounding hooves filled the night air. The dark shadows were gaining on them.

"Faster," Johann shouted to Anna. "Faster."

Miraculously the horses gained speed. Then Anna veered to the right, down another road. The road was muddier, more dangerous for the horses, but it was a risk they had to take. They had to keep going and urged their mounts on. Time stood still as they raced in the darkness.

At one point, the pursuers had almost caught up; he could feel the breath of their horses, but then one of them had stumbled—giving them another advantage to pull ahead.

Unexpectedly Anna slowed down. Johann was forced to do the same. He wondered if she knew what she was doing. Then she slowed even more as she turned her horse sharply to the left, and down a lane.

Johann recognized the lane; it was the home stretch. Did they have enough of a lead to give them time to get into the house? Would Boris be home? What state of mind would he be in?

The answer came with one crack of a rifle, and a bullet whizzing past them.

"Boris!" Anna shrieked. "It's us."

Another bullet whizzed by them.

"Boris!" Anna continued to scream. "It's Anna and Johann. Help us! Open the door!"

Two more shots rang out. They were only warning shot. But there were curses coming from behind them. The sound of chasing hooves stopped.

Johann turned—there were only two horsemen and he realized that these wasn't Vladimir and his men but two common Russian thieves taking advantage of travelers in the night.

Anna continued to scream at Boris. The rifle stopped firing. Finally, the horses came to a sliding, muddy halt at the front of the house.

Anna slid down into the mud, clutching her knapsack, as the front door was flung open. She ran inside. Johann was at her heels, turning to slam the door behind them.

"How many?" Boris asked.

"Two," Johann said breathlessly.

"Same ones who hurt Nadia?" asked Anna.

"No," answered Johann, "I thought it was them, but there were only two of them the last time I checked and the horses were the type owned by the Russian peasants."

"But they still have it coming," Boris said, opening the door a crack and sticking his rifle through it, and continuing to fire. The dogs were standing on guard barking.

Then Boris pulled in his rifle, and listened.

Nothing.

They were safe—this house was like a fortress.

Anna looked at Johann and he shrugged. "For tonight we are safe."

The dogs were barking again.

"Probably wolves," Boris muttered, throwing open the door. "Canon, come in here."

Canon barked in response, a bark of delight at the call of his master.

Boris closed the door with a slam and slumped against it.

Then Boris straightened. "Anna, take a candle and get me more ammunition from the kitchen pantry, the back cupboard. Johann and I need to stand guard," Boris said. "Even though they are gone for now—one never knows."

Johann and Anna glanced at each other knowingly. Boris was now in battle mode and would play it out until the morning—most likely.

Anna lit a candle and crept to the pantry at the back of the house. She opened the back cupboard and gasped. There were enough rifles and bullets in the cupboard to arm a battalion. It wasn't as if she wasn't used to guns; everyone had guns in the village. Hunting was common. It was the amount and the variety.

She carried as much as she could back to the front door, wondering what she was really doing. She was Mennonite, helping an armed man shoot.

She gave a rifle to Johann. "It doesn't hurt to shoot into the air," she said.

"They're going to wait this one out," said Boris, leaning back. "We might as well get some pillows, some blankets, and I'll take the first watch."

Anne went to find the blankets and pillows. When she came back, Boris and Johann were resting on the sofas in the living room. Boris had lit the evening lanterns.

Then Boris, still checking the guns, asked. "So both of you might tell me what this is all about."

They told him. He nodded and smiled. He loved the idea of a cache of jewelry. "Do you have the books along?"

Anna pulled them out of her bag. "Yes, I do."

"Why don't you read to us, Anna, and tell us what you think?"

Anna snuggled down into her corner and opened up the Bible. "My mother wrote down references and names beside them. My name has Psalms 94:19 beside it. There is a reference for Aaron, for her first husband, Menno, and for, Viktor."

There was a long silence.

"It was Viktor, wasn't it?"

Johann nodded.

"The reference beside Viktor's name is Philippians 4:10." Anna paged to the passage in the Bible. *I know what it is to be in need and I know what it is to have plenty. I have learned the secret of being content in any and every situation, whether well fed or hungry.... Not that I'm looking for a gift, but I am looking for what may be credited to your account. I have received full payment and even more.... I have received from Epaphroditus the gift you sent.*

Anna paused, "...and here's a note in her handwriting—which I've read many times, but it never made sense to me before—now I wonder if it's a clue. *Gifts in the chest of hymnals in the church, in the safe.*"

Johann burst out laughing. "There it is. That wasn't difficult at all. You know the chest of hymnals at the church—it has a false bottom, I'm sure. Most do." He took the Bible and reread the message and the passage. "This is it. I'm sure of it."

Boris chuckled. "In the morning you can take the horses—make your way round the back to the church and find us our treasure. We will be rich."

Anna was dismayed to see the light in his eyes. He was feeling ownership. "This isn't our money or our jewels. It is a curse," she said getting up, suddenly feeling very tired. "I'm going to go to sleep."

"Yes, do that," Boris agreed. "I'll check the grounds one more time. Then lock up. But I think we are safe."

"I'll sleep here on the sofa." Johann said grabbing a pillow and a throw blanket.

"There is a spare bedroom upstairs next to Anna's," Boris offered.

The moment was suddenly tense—as they both remembered the kiss—the instant passion.

"I'll sleep down here," Johann said firmly.

Chapter FOURTEEN

It was a restless sleep. It seemed as if she had spent the entire night trying to process the day—trying to make sense of this crazy scavenger hunt of her mother's making, the chase, the kiss, the shooting and now another anticipated trip back to the village. Maybe she would let the men go and find the jewelry and she could spend the day reading in the library of this amazing house.

Anna went through the closet and found a beautiful but very plain durable traveling dress. She was hungry.

She found Boris and Johann in the breakfast each quietly eating a bowl of porridge. Boris looked remarkably rested. Johann looked tired.

An elderly woman served her a bowl at the table, poured her a cup of coffee and then disappeared without a word. This was the phantom housekeeper....

"We need to leave soon," Boris said quietly. "My guns are packed."

Anna groaned. She hadn't expected Boris to join them though it made sense that he thought they would need protection. She noticed the gun on the table. How had it come to this?

Suddenly there was a loud knock at the back kitchen door. Both Johann and Boris flew into action. But before they could answer it, the door burst open and a man stood there in full uniform.

Boris saw only the uniform and raised his gun. "Don't move."

It was Mikhail. Seeing the gun, he raised his hand in a gesture of friendliness but Boris saw only the threat—took aim and fired.

Simultaneously, Johann swung his body to ward off the gun shot and took the bullet in his shoulder while Anna jumped and grabbed Boris' gun and wrenched it from him screaming. "Boris its Mikhail—he's on our side a good man!"

Reeling in pain, Johann slumped onto the floor. Blood throbbed from his wound, soaking his shirt—leaving red puddles of blood on the floor.

Boris knelt down to examine Johann's wound carefully. He was still on the battlefield. "Bullet went through—flesh wound only," he announced to Anna as he took off his own shirt, ripped it into strips, and pressed it against the wound to make it stop bleeding. When it soaked through almost immediately, he tied on another, and another, until he was certain that the pressure of his bandages would stop the bleeding.

Together the three of them, Anna, Mikhail and Boris carried Johann to the bed in the spare bedroom on the first floor where they made him as comfortable as they could. They took off his shirt and cleansed the wound. By this time, he was trembling with shock—then they covered him with thick blankets.

Boris managed to pour something he called "medicinal" down his throat, and soon Johann was closing his eyes—either unconscious or mercifully in a deep sleep.

Downstairs in the kitchen again, Boris served Mikhail a quick breakfast of cold porridge, coffee and fruit, while Anna described to Mikhail what had happened the day before—the midafternoon visit with Neufeld that uncovered a promise of a hidden clue in her mother's Bible or book. The hope of this led them to going back to her house to find the copy of the Bible and the novel. But then as they were returning to Neufeld's, how they were ambushed by the three rebels that sent them on a chase through the storm ending here, taking refuge at the estate—with Boris, the great defender.

Mikhail smiled. "The right place—Boris is a great defender."

Anna continued describing that how once they were settled in the living room they had actually gone through the Bible and found a clue that suggested "gifts" were hidden in a hymnal box at the church.

"So, if I understand you correctly," Mikhail leaned forward. "Neufeld is still waiting for an answer and does not know about the clue in the Bible that suggests the jewels might be hidden in a hymnal box at the church?"

Anna nodded.

"And we don't know where Vladimir and his gang are now—and how much they know?"

Anna nodded.

Kamensky stared at her. "Amazing." Then he leaned back - thoughtfully. "Why don't you stay here—look after Johann and I'll go back and fetch a doctor. Meanwhile I will visit Neufeld, show him the Bible, see if the jewels are actually at the church in the hymnal box—and then come back here. I think Johann is stable. I think we have time for this." He shook his head in disgust. "We have to stop this warring nonsense for everyone's peace of mind," he glanced at Boris who was busy with another bowl of porridge.

Anna nodded. "But before you go—why did you come here in the first place?"

He laughed.... "Perhaps I shouldn't have come.... given Johann's injury. Someone could have died."

"Seriously...."

"When you didn't come home last night, we were all sick with worry—so we were combing the streets—searching all night. Early this morning someone tipped us off that they had heard that there were two thieves who had encountered a couple in the storm who had outraced them and escaped into a yard whose owner had a gun. They thought it was Boris' estate and he was the owner with the gun."

"Really...."

Mikhail smiled. "It was one of the more reliable sources I have so I came immediately to check it out… not expecting to startle you—but save you."

He got up. "Now I must really go and report back to everyone. They are concerned…."

"Stay safe," Anna murmured trying to process it all.

Kamensky disappeared through the same door he had come. Minutes later they heard a horse galloping off the yard.

For the rest of the morning, Anna could not pry herself away from Johann's bedside. She was content to watch Johann sleep, to stay by his side, and stroke his hand. She would always be grateful he had survived the gun wound. The fact that he had so selflessly thrown himself in front of Boris to save Mikhail's life was the bravest thing she had ever seen.

It didn't matter anymore what his opinion of her was; he could vote to have her excommunicated but she would care for him always. She pondered the kiss—it had made her feel alive—guilty—but alive. Was it love? If it was love—it was forbidden. He was taken…. And he disapproved of her. He could never love her—the kiss was proof of that. There was something between them but it could not be allowed.

Noticing that he was beginning to flush, she felt his forehead; he was running a fever. She called for Boris. "We have to do something for him!" she demanded almost hysterically." We need a doctor."

"Not to worry," Boris said. "He's a strong young man. He'll pull through."

But Anna watched Johann intently, breathing with him and for him. This man—who disdained her yet had protected her from the thieves—had to live.

Around noon, Anna found her way back to the kitchen

"You look absolutely dreadful, Anna," Boris said disgustedly. "Look at yourself. Your hair is a mess. Your clothes are bloodied. Go change your dress, freshen up and then come and have lunch with me in the library," he said. This time it was an order.

Reluctantly she went to the bedroom she had claimed as her own. She dropped her blood-stained dress onto the floor, forced herself to pour water from the pitcher into the bowl, and wash her face, her neck, and her legs. She pulled out a dark, loose fitting, burgundy dress with bits of lace floating down the bodice and around the neck from the closet and put it on. She combed out her hair and let it hang loose, too tired to put it up. Then she glanced at her reflection in the mirror. Nothing could disguise the tired hollow look of her eyes, the drained pallor on her cheeks.

Grabbing a sweater, she went back to the kitchen. Boris had reheated some borscht.

"Sit," he said, guiding her to the easy chair beside the fire. "You're also trembling," he observed quietly.

Her hands were trembling so much she couldn't trust herself to eat. She sipped the juice he offered her and felt it burn its way down her throat, warming her as nothing else could.

Boris watched her. Then said softly. "Anna—you and your mother are remarkable—and I do believe that if we are here—it means we are here for a purpose. There is a reason you are here in my house. I've been trying to piece this whole thing together. Mighty strange. That was Viktor's boy wasn't it, the man who took the Bible and shot Johann?"

Anna was shocked—in some confused way Boris had made Mikhail the person who had shot Johann.

"Yes, that was Mikhail Kamensky from St. Petersburg," Anna said. Boris could be so capable one day and absolutely helpless the next. Obviously, he thrived on excitement. His eyes had more clarity than she had ever seen before.

"That would be Viktor Kamensky's son," he nodded to himself.

"I don't know who he is," she said watching twiddle his thumbs.

"And these jewels were Viktor's, given to Elizabeth for safekeeping, but are now wanted by both the Tsar and the rebels," he summarized, obviously relishing the intrigue in which he found himself.

She raised her eyebrows. "Does it make sense to you?"

He nodded. "I don't think they're going to find the jewels in the church."

Anna froze. "And why not?"

"Oh, they might find another brooch or pin or something—but not all of it."

"And why not?" she asked, again hoping he was delusional.

"Because your mother wouldn't hide the jewels in the church. That would have been Viktor's plan. He would have told her to hide them in the sanctuary of the church, right?"

Anna nodded. She had no idea where he was going with this.

"But Elizabeth wouldn't see the church as safe."

"And why not?"

"Do you feel safe in a church?'

Anna studied her food. No—she didn't feel safe in church. It was full of damnation—except of course when Neufeld spoke.

Boris read her silence. "Like you, Anna, your mother lived by her heart. When you have something you love, where do you keep it? In your brother's room?"

Anna thought of the tin box she hid in the hay mow. "No." She had picked a place where the fresh scent of straw, the dusty sunbeams shining through the cracks in the wood, and the quietness always made her feel safe.

"You don't keep it in your room either because that's where people would look."

Anna nodded.

"So where do you keep it? In a place you like to go to but where no one will suspect."

Anna nodded. Now she understood.

"Elizabeth, your mother, didn't always like to go to church. She went to meet her friends, to hear Neufeld speak, but she said she had no voice in your church."

Anna nodded. In an odd way he was making sense. Even though her mother attended church regularly, she would take every opportunity to miss if she had a good excuse, and go only to meet her friends. She liked Neufeld's sermons, but often said she worshiped God in the kitchen.

"Your heart shrivels in a place where it has no voice."

Anna nodded, though she knew there was something very dangerous and threatening to her entire community in those words.

"So where did she hide the jewels?" Boris cut through her thoughts. "I think you're right when you say that your mother, Elizabeth, probably wrote everything down in her journals. But that clue has been burned. All the usual clues are gone."

"If it's not in the Bible—we're back to the beginning. The secret is lost; the jewels are lost forever," she wailed.

"No, Anna. I think you know."

"I don't know!" Anna exclaimed. How often did she have to scream out those words before anyone would listen to her and leave her alone?

"Here, let me fill your glass. Take another drink of your juice." He was smiling wickedly, with a twinkle in his eyes.

She took another sip. And another. It was becoming increasingly less important what anyone thought.

"Where did your mother give you the Fabergé pin, Anna? Think back to that day, and remember every detail. Visualize it in your mind, and describe it to me."

Anna closed her eyes and leaned into the chair. For the first time in days, she actually felt safe. Even her body, which had been aching with the pain of the stallion's kick, the walking, and the night's travels, was soothed, warm and comfortable. Her eyelids felt unbearably heavy, the perfect dark backdrop for what she was imagining.

"I remember the day. We had come here to your place, to pick up some books. I think it was the Anna Karenina book.

You and she had been discussing it at length. I think I fell asleep right here in the library before the fire, while you talked and talked about it. I remember my mother calling it the best love story. You were saying something about her not marrying the Mayor and then you said something about a man from St. Petersburg.

"Later in the day—it was a warm day—my mother said that we should go for a walk. She was carrying a bag. I thought we were going to the railway tracks for a picnic. My mother liked the place where the river and the tracks were close. There's this special place, a little hill, blueberry bushes, a shed, some old railway ties, and a big abandoned train wheel. She liked that wheel. One time she even planted daisies right in the middle of the rim.

"I was wearing a black dress, with white lace. She made a wreath of daisies for both of us. She was wearing a black dress too. Then she told me to go and play for a bit—she had to do something. There was a tiny pond, puddle really, that I liked to play in. I took some leaves and floated them in the pond. I took my shoes off and waded in the warm water.

"Then she called for me. We sat down on a rock. The sun was warm. And then she gave me the pin. She had one too. I don't know where that one went. Hers was all gold and diamonds. She said mine was a special gift and that I should never show anyone.

"I didn't. Even though I was little, I never told anyone. I think I loved it too much. I think I believed that if anyone knew about it they would want it, and I loved it too much to share with anyone."

"And what about the bag—was it a picnic lunch?"

Anna shook her head. "I don't remember seeing the bag again."

Boris' face was close. "Do you remember where this special place is?"

Chapter FIFTEEN

Mikhail raced down the river road to Neufeld's house. It seemed to be taking less time. He had found a short cut.

Neufeld's wife answered the door to tell him that her husband had been called away to tend to a death bed request. He had left a message that Mikhail seek Loepky's help if he needed anything from the church leadership.

He found Loepky at his home in the middle of hiring yet another guard to keep his horse safe, which had miraculously returned in the night. He had been elated. The Russian peasant was nodding, hat in hand, listening intently to Loepky's warnings of punishment and damnation if anything should again befall this precious animal.

"Give it up," Kamensky said, striding into the room. "If they want to take it, they will."

Loepky was horrified. "Not if I have one of their own guarding it."

Mikhail smiled. "Oh—right," he said, rolling his eyes. "But I have something much more important for you to consider." He held out the Bible.

This time it was Loepky's turn to roll his eyes. "A Bible? I didn't expect this from you."

"The jewels. We have finally found some clues as to the whereabouts of the jewels!" Mikhail said, a little exasperated. He didn't much care for this man.

"The reference is Philippians 4:10." Loepky paged to the passage in the Bible. *I know what it is to be in need and I know what it is to have plenty. I have learned the secret of being content in any and every situation, whether well fed or hungry.... Not that I'm looking for a gift, but I am looking for what may be credited to your account. I have received full payment and even more.... I have received from Epaphroditus the gift you sent.*

Mikhail pointed to the note. *Gift is in the chest of hymnals in the church, in the safe.*

Loepky burst into a smile. "This is it? Who would have thought it would be under the chest of hymnals. It has a false bottom I'm sure.... Let's go have us a look."

It wasn't far to walk, and the church wasn't locked.

It was still cool inside the church.

Mikhail was again astounded how simple the inside of the building was. Outside it looked plain, but he had expected that—these people lived simple lives. But he thought that because they valued their faith, they would put more emphasis on their place of worship. But there were no stained-glass windows—no sculptures of their Jesus on a cross—nothing.

Loepky led him straight to the box, a chest really, handmade, pine. Large, with a lid that looked worn from being sat on. There was nothing holy about this chest.

"The settlers, our ancestors, brought this box on the first trip here filled with church books, hymnals, Bibles, sermon notes."

"Is it ever locked?"

Loepky smiled. "No…." He started to dig out the books quickly. Mikhail watched. The books looked worn, old.

Once he had reached the bottom, Loepky examined the box closely." I don't think there is a false bottom."

"Let's turn it around."

Now that it was empty, it was fairly easy to turn the box around and look at the backside. There, hardly distinguishable, were the faint lines of a hidden compartment—a false bottom drawer.

Mikhail bent down and pulled it ever so slightly. It moved. He pulled it out further, very aware that Loepky was breathing shallowly.

He opened the drawer slowly. It creaked, moved with some difficulty as if it hadn't been moved in a very long time. Only he could really see the contents. There was one pin, brooch, almost identical to Anna's. This was definitely one of the hiding places, but there was nothing else.

Mikhail reached down and took out the pin.

"The jewel is here." He held the pin up against the sun. "This will fetch a pretty penny."

Loepky took the beautiful brooch from Mikhail to examine it, and then gave it back. His disappointment palatable.

"Amateur," thought Mikhail. There had been moments during this visit when he had been tempted to rediscover his mother's past, to perhaps explore what it meant to be truly Mennonite. When he saw Neufeld, Anna, even Johann, he was tempted to become one of them—to leave the Russian world and settle down here.

They didn't know that—none of them.

They also didn't know that he was actually one of them. He was Martha's son. His mother, Martha, and his father, Viktor, had kept his birth a secret from these people thinking they might want to claim him—so none of them knew.

And what none of them suspected was how his father had taken the shunning of Martha as a personal rejection. He had truly loved Martha. What no one knew was that after Martha's early death that love had been transferred to Elizabeth which is why they had remained secretly connected even after Martha's death. Even Elizabeth didn't know the depth of his love and trust he had in her. He suspected that another reason for all of this was that his father had found God here. He had often attended church here—first of all because of Martha and then because of his own change of heart. He had even tried to live out his beliefs as a Russian—never quite feeling he succeeded.

Of course, growing up as a child of this man, he had understood none of this, had even reacted to what he considered the "soft" side of his father and joined the army to prove his point. Yet secretly he had admired his father.

Now after his father's death he found himself grieving more than he could ever have imagined. He now also regretted that he hadn't learned more about this God that gave those who believed in him—truly believed in him—this wonderful aura of peace, wisdom and love.

Loepky gave the brooch back. His eyes black.

"Amateur," Mikhail returned to the only word that could describe Loepky. Most greedy men knew to hide their deceit better than this man.

He was truly disgusted. After he had met Loepky during that first meeting, he had realized what the man was, he knew he could never be part of a community who held the man in esteem. They were all fools.

Mikhail turned and walked out of the church. Now he needed to find a doctor.

Boris' face was close. "Do you remember the place?" He asked again.

"Yes," Anna answered.

"Then we are going for a walk."

"I can't leave Johann. In fact, I should go look on him now.

Just then they heard the sound of horses. Boris immediately went on alert. Anna looked out of her window. "It's Aaron and Nadia."

Anna ran to the front door to greet them, her exuberance short lived when she saw Nadia's obvious vulnerability. She still looked like one huge bruise as she winced getting off the horse. Needing to be assisted up the front stairs and settled into a chair.

After Aaron looked after the horses, he came inside delighted that lunch was being served.

Once they were settled at the table set with buns, cold meats and a plate of bubliki, butter and fresh cream, with of course the "medicinal" juice.

After a quick prayer, Anna was first to ask the obvious. "Why did you bring Nadia here? She's hurting."

Aaron shrugged. "When we heard from Kamensky that you were here, she insisted on being with you—and there is no stopping Nadia when she wants something." He heaped his plate high. "Now you explain what has been happening."

As Anna began to describe the day, she realized how little he knew about the jewels, the scavenger hunt, the chase last night and the latest development of Johann being shot.

She noticed that even though Nadia seemed half asleep, barely able to eat the bun in her hand she, was paying attention.

After a very quick lunch they settled Nadia in her room, and Anna took Aaron to check up on Johann.

Aaron responded well to Johann's needs—checking the bandages—assessing the wound with an expertise Anna had been unaware of.

"Mikhail is coming with a doctor," Anna told him.

"And now," Boris said, standing at the door watching the exchange, "you and I are going for a walk to the river."

Anna arched her eyebrows. "We are? We have guests!"

"Aaron can look after Johann and Nadia." He said curtly. "You and I are going to walk."

Anna sighed, when Boris was determined, there was no sense trying to dissuade him. Perhaps it was best to do it now before Mikhail came back. It was true Aaron could look after Johann and Nadia.

"Go," said Aaron—eyeing the grand piano "I need a distraction. I will play for the sick."

She took her sweater. "Boris, you're not going to take any of your rifles—are you?" The thought of walking with Boris, armed, was becoming terrifying for her.

"I'm always armed," he said, "We are going to retrace the exact steps you and your mother took the day she gave you her pin. And I want you to describe the way it was."

"You old sneak," she smiled. "You don't for a minute think that the jewels have been found. Yet you didn't tell Aaron and Nadia?"

He grunted. "We don't really know for certain, do we?"

Anna stepped out the door.

It was a glorious day. The night rain had left everything fresh and green. The warmth embraced them.

"I don't think we are going to need sweaters," Anna said, slipping hers off.

"Take it along, you never know," Boris said pointing towards the Caucasus mountains already covered with a fringe of dark clouds. "You never know."

They walked to the edge of the yard, arm in arm. "This is the way we walked," laughed Anna, feeling playful and free. "At the edge of your yard, we would look back to see if you were alright. You'd be standing on the stairs waving to us—and we would wave back.

"Then we would duck down into this trail. The minute we were out of sight, my mother would take in a deep breath, something like this." She imitated her mother. "We are alone and free," she always said.

"Then she would walk—her hands touching the leaves as we passed, her eyes scanning the scenery constantly. Sometimes she would point out the birds, special flowers, and always she would say how wonderful it was to be in nature. It was as if she was partaking of a special meal and constantly needing to comment on how delicious it all was."

Boris smiled. "Your mother lived intensely."

They walked in silence. The shade of the trees made it feel cooler; Anna slipped her sweater back on. Boris took out a cigarette and lit it, smoking as he went. Sometimes he hummed to himself.

It was a peaceful walk. After everything they had gone through it seemed odd to take this interlude and enter into something so different; yet it felt so right. The nightmare chase the night before, the fear of being beaten, the fear of her stepmother, were all gone now. So much had changed in these last few days. Something important had happened, was happening to her. She knew that she could never go back to being the person she was before. For one thing, she could not go and live under the tyrannical rule of her stepmother. It was over. And she could not leave Nadia behind. Poor Nadia. She would need months to heal. And there was also Johann....

Boris led the way up a hill. "Are you sure this is the way that your mother came? I've never noticed the rabbit trail—we usually come through here on the wider path with the horses."

Anna nodded. "My mother liked to find her own places." She paused when they reached the top.

"I haven't been here for a long while," he said looking around. "It is quite lovely with the river, the valley, and then that cliff of sorts."

She nodded. "It gets even nicer."

They followed the river for a while, often sitting down to rest exactly where she and her mother had rested. "Remember I was a little girl then," Anna explained. "Sometimes when the berries were out, my mother would pick berries while I rested."

Boris nodded. "Your mother used to come here even before you were born," he said softly.

"Really?"

"I had no idea where she went of course. My wife and I were usually busy, and never felt that we should intrude on her personal time. Sometimes my wife went with her…."

"Why did she come?"

"I think she met someone out here."

"Martha perhaps…." Anna nodded. "I remember her saying that sometimes. It was their favorite place to be together. Especially after Martha was excommunicated from the church. They had to meet in secret. It is part of the shunning practice."

Boris nodded. "That would make sense. We are coming close to a station here. If someone were coming in from St. Petersburg—this would make a natural place to meet. I'm beginning to understand. I never thought I was an accomplice to this kind of thing. If I had known about the jewels, my goodness—this would have been solved a long time ago." He was smiling.

"And what would you have done with all that money?" Anna asked, laughing sarcastically. "Buy a big house, buy more horses, give your wife more dresses?"

He smiled. "You're right. Most of life's problems can't be solved with money." He sat down again, on a big boulder, taking out another cigarette.

She sat down beside him. She had never seen him like this, so calm, so clear. She wanted to hold onto the moment for him as well as for her.

"How far?"

"Just over there. Around that hill. There's another tiny rabbit trail that we can follow. There is a lagoon surrounded by hills, rocks. In the spring when the river is swollen, the lagoon is fed with fresh water, but by summer it shrinks to a puddle. I suspect that it will be full now after the rain."

"This whole area is lovely," Boris commented. "Just lovely," he said standing up. "Next time, we'll take a horse," he said. "This walking is hard work."

Finally, they saw the lagoon. It was midafternoon.

"This is it," Anna said running to the water, taking off her shoes and wading into it. Suddenly she was ten years old again. The rain had swollen the lagoon.

"Where did she go when you were playing?" Boris asked.

Anna paused—she remembered. They had come here for a purpose this time, and it wasn't to play.

Anna stepped out of the water, slipped into her shoes again. "She would walk this way."

Anna started to walk. She had never walked into his direction, but she remembered the sound of her mother's steps. Trying to be her mother, she walked along a short trail, into the shadow of a cliff. She could almost hear her mother's heartbeat. Then she noticed that the rocks turned into steps as they climbed up the cliff, and then before her was a crack in the cliff. Odd.

Boris let out a whistle. "This is amazing," he said. "From any distance, no one would ever suspect that this crevice was here. Shelter from the rain too."

Anna stepped into the shadow of the crack in the rock. It was large enough for one person, two if they squeezed, as happened when Boris followed her in.

"See," he was saying. "See, I knew you could do it. Now where would she hide the jewels?"

He stepped back, giving her space. "Think—where would you hide a box of jewels?"

She turned slowly around and around in the little space. Then she put her arm up; her fingers found a narrow ledge.

"Here," she said. "And there is nothing."

"Stretch," Boris said. "You are somewhat shorter than your mother."

She stretched. Her fingers touched something smooth. She held her breath. She stretched more till her fingers could encircle the box. Then slowly she withdrew it from its hidden place. Bringing it into the light, she gazed at it in wonder. It was a tin box much like the box that had held the diaries, much like the box that had held her Bible and Tolstoy novel. This was definitely her mother's.

Boris stepped aside. "Take it into the sunlight" he said. "Here is a tree stump… let's look."

Her hands were shaking as she laid the box on her lap. She looked up at Boris. He was standing, watching her, rifle in hand.

"You think this is it?" she asked.

"Yes," he said.

She smiled. "It could be more books, more journals, even pictures."

She tried to lift the lid; it was stuck. She pulled harder, and it flipped open, half spilling its contents onto her lap. Nothing could have prepared her for the sight of the jewels, diamonds, sapphires, rubies, and gold lying on a black velvet cloth. Their beauty was breathtaking.

"*Blin!*" Boris swore.

She looked up, confused at his response." Isn't this a good thing? To have found them?" She held up a diamond-studded necklace against the sun, her fingers caressing it lightly.

He shook his head. "Look at you. It's already working; it's demon magic on you. This stuff brings out the demons in everyone."

She laughed. "Here, you can have this ring. It has this wonderful diamond. It suits you perfectly, dear nobleman."

He shook his head. "I won't touch the stuff."

She laughed. "I'm going to enjoy this," she said, trying on a ruby ring.

At that very moment, a huge cloud hid the sun from them. The valley became almost dark. Anna shivered; it was an ominous sign. What if these jewels were cursed?

Chapter SIXTEEN

Johann heard a scream and then another. It was Nadia, he was sure of it. He listened intently. There were harsh voices, chairs scraping against a floor, banging cupboard doors and then more muffled screams.

He tried to move; his mind was still foggy. It took him quite a while to remember everything that had happened. His sore shoulder was the first sharp reminder. Vaguely he remembered he had been shot. He remembered Boris forcing firewater down his throat, probably the "medicinal" juice, which had helped—so much so it was still clouding his mind. His body felt like lead, his shoulder like red-hot molten lava, with searing pain every time he tried to move.

What was Nadia doing here? he wondered. How long had he slept? Why was she screaming? Slowly he remembered. Mikhail had taken the Bible; something must have gone wrong. Were they back already? If so, it meant that they had been wrong with the clue to the treasure. If they hadn't found it, the revolutionaries would be more desperate, in a fouler mood than before. Where was Anna? Boris?

He slid off the bed onto the floor. The effort left him dizzy with pain. Slowly he inched to the door, not making a sound. Through a crack in the floor, he could see Vladimir; Nadia was against the cupboard.

Aaron was lying unconscious between them on the floor.

"Talk, you bitch."

Nadia seemed frozen with fear. "I saw them—walking."

"Where were they going?"

Nadia hesitated too long and was punched in the ribs, still broken from the last time. She gasped, and moaned.

"I know—," she whispered hoarsely. She was gulping, struggling to breathe. "I can—show—."

"Do they have the gems?"

"They think…." She was nodding painfully.

Vladimir stepped back to address the others. "I think I know what's happening here. Anna and Boris know the real hiding place. While they sent us on a wild goose chase, they were scheming here to find the real place."

"Right? Nadia?" he screamed in her face. "They think they know?"

There were tears streaming down her face as she again nodded painfully. "I heard them—talking," she whispered, sucking in air whenever she could.

"What about Johann?"

"Shot...." She shook her head. "Almost—dead? Mikhail is coming back with a doctor."

"Mikhail? Shouldn't we look after him first?" asked one of the men hidden from Johann's view.

"No," said Vladimir, "we can get the jewels and be out of here before he comes to. Speed here is important. You two take Nadia, put her on a horse, and keep her conscious. We need her."

Johann drew back and leaned against the wall as he heard them leave. Anna and Boris were out there, probably not realizing the rebels were after them, and Nadia was going to betray them all. He could already feel his body trembling from the exertion of crawling across the floor. What could he do?

He stood up, wincing every time he moved. He could feel the shot pierce his shoulder again and again, each time inflicting incredible pain. He hobbled down the stair and made his way to the kitchen window to see where they were going. They were all on horseback, heading down a trail.

Somehow, he managed to get himself into the barn, where he forced himself to saddle a horse. Three times he tried to heave the saddle over the back of the horse; three times he almost fainted, needing to put his head down to bring some blood back into his woozy head. He was disgusted with himself.

He had been diminished to nothing, a wounded piece of meat, hugging a horse for dear life. How was he supposed to save Anna in this condition? He saw the ridiculousness of it, but couldn't stop himself.

Perhaps he couldn't ride but he could walk. Perhaps he could cry out a warning. Perhaps he might fling himself in the way of an attack. He had sustained one bullet, why not another? He needed to protect Anna!

He was hot and delirious. He saw images of flying beasts hovering over him, glowing green eyes, giant snapping mouths, wet fangs glittering in the sunlight. The beasts were also in his head.

His body ached to stop but he couldn't. He would not. He made it to the far edge of the yard and then it all went black.

Nadia saw nothing of the countryside as they rode along the trail. Only occasionally, when they came to a fork in the trail, someone would jostle her into consciousness and ask her where they were. She would force herself to open her eyes, and ascertain which direction to take.

She reluctantly leaned against her abductor needing his strong body as a brace against the torturous rhythm of the horse. Every bump and every unexpected jolt sent excruciating tremors through her body. She could barely hold on—it was all unfocussed, black and horrid.

She was betraying Anna—that was her real agony. She was leading her three captors to the sacred place that Elizabeth had always called "blessed."

Shortly after Nadia had joined the family, the three of them, Anna's mother had taken her to this spot off the main river path, as hallow lagoon surrounded by hills and large boulders, where they would spend an afternoon together, swimming, climbing or just basking in the sun. Elizabeth was so taken with this place; she had insisted on visiting it regularly.

When Nadia was a child, it had just been a place where she had learned to swim with her brothers—and where they could hide from their parents. It had one strong advantage—still did. Most of the neighboring community avoided the place. Most thought the place was haunted by a ghost or voracious animal because of the mutilated body of a man that had been found in the lagoon a long time ago. These stories had never scared her nor her brothers, and they certainly had never frightened Elizabeth. "We don't believe in things like that," she would sniff with disgust.

Nadia stiffened, and felt her cracked ribs shift painfully. She had to stop. She couldn't take these men to that place. It would betray Anna—and to betray Anna would mean death to her own soul. She knew that. To stop would mean another kind of death. Either way it meant death, so why not stop? Why not submit to fate?

Yet she couldn't stop. If anyone, Anna would know how to deal with this. Anna with her friends would be able to stop this.... The black ink spots were growing, the windy darkness in her mind was absorbing her, controlling her, and she couldn't stop.

None of it made sense, except that she was desperate to live, desperate to see Anna one more time, desperate to see how this would end.

She wanted to scream out her agony, but she clenched her teeth to contain the pain. Later she would scream.

Anna stared at the box filled with jewels. She felt a series of icy shivers run up and down her spine. This was more than just a tin box of gaudy trinkets. This was worth millions of rubles. People went mad over the sight of so much wealth. Boris was well aware of it. She saw a look of blind terror take root in his eyes.

"What do we do now?" Anna asked, closing the box.

The jewels were beginning to play with his mind. Boris' eyes were beginning to focus on the imaginary demons. He was gripping his gun.

This is what Anna feared most. "Boris, stay with me."

But he was becoming another person, a warrior, and a soldier on the battlefield, sensing danger and living by his wits. "You stay here," he said in a hushed tone. "I think someone is coming," he said, rushing into the underbrush.

"No Boris!" she screamed. "No one is coming."

Then she hesitated. What if someone was coming? What should she do?

She paused, remembering her mother. Then she opened the box again. She took out two pins and one ring and slipped them into her pocket. Then she took out four of the largest necklaces and wrapped them in the velvet cloth. It didn't look as if she had even made a dent in the treasure. There was enough treasure here for everyone.

Then she hid the tin box just outside the cavern behind a rock, and covered it with a pile of leaves. She would come back for it, once she knew it was safe. She went to find Boris.

Boris was zigzagging down to the lagoon, dodging imaginary bullets. "Got to get ready," he was grumbling. He took a shot at the top of a tree. "There, that will keep them off for a bit."

But the shot echoed and reechoed off the stones. Anna groaned. It was hardly a warning at this point; it was a signal to everyone far and near that indicated exactly where they were, and an invitation to join the action.

"Don't, Boris. Please don't shoot," she called to him. "There is no one here. Why don't we go back, just you and I?" She ran after him, pulling on his arm, but he would have none of it.

"Missy, you leave me alone. There's a war going on here," he said as he ran down a trail leading to the railway tracks, disappearing in seconds.

There was no sense in running after him. He was out of sight before she could say his name. She made her way back to the treasure.

Then she heard someone calling her name from the opposite direction. Anna whirled around.

She saw someone on horseback coming towards her. It was Nadia.

"Anna," Nadia called.

Anna froze in her tracks. Nadia? Out here? And then she saw that there was a man doubling on her horse, sitting in her shadow. Emerging out of the bushes were two more riders.

She knew immediately that they were the three rebels.

Vladimir moved to the front. The rider holding Nadia fell back.

"Finally, we meet, Anna." Vladimir slid off his shores, pointing a gun at her. "You know why we're here."

Anna nodded. "I have them for you," she said. Holding out the velvet cloth, she unfolded it slowly. "Here," she said. "Take them, and leave my friend alone." She could feel her fingers trembling, her heart in her throat.

One of the men was holding a knife to Nadia's throat.

"I also want the ones you've taken for yourself," he said. "Give me all the jewels or Nadia dies."

Anna pulled out the gems from her pocket.

He laughed with delight. "I knew that you'd take some for yourself."

Anna stood still, waiting for the jubilation to subside.

Vladimir let the necklace of diamonds ripple through his fingers. "This will finance the entire revolution." He was grinning. "We can celebrate tonight." He just stood there transfixed, admiring them, holding them to the light, and displaying them against his dirty shirt, hypnotized by their beauty.

He was actually drooling over the jewels. "My precious jewels," he was saying again and again, intoxicated by their beauty.

Chapter SEVENTEEN

At the sound of voices, Mikhail slid off his horse and tied it to a tree.

He hid behind one tree—and then another staying out of sight.

For one moment, he paused to study the landscape ascertaining the best approach to take.

He was tired. It had been a long day. It was as if he was always one step behind. It truly had been one wild goose chase.

First of all, hearing from Slevkov, the bar tender at the tavern, about Vladimir and his goons chasing Johann and Anna until they lost them in the storm last night. Then from another source that Johanna and Anna had landed up at Boris.

He had made his way to the estate immediately only to be shot at by deranged Boris and saved by Johann leaving him badly wounded. Then, after being hearing the story of the clue in the Bible, he had gone to the village to inform Neufeld only to meet up with Loepky and find a symbolic piece of jewelry in the chest of hymnals.

Then he had stopped at the village doctor Mark Froese—even had to bribe him to come and accompany him all the way to Boris' estate only to find Aaron unconscious on the floor in the house. And then tracing a trail of blood to find Johann at the edge of the yard unconscious. With the help of the doctor Froese had carried him back to his bed where he had gained enough consciousness to brief them on Nadia and the three rebels.

This trail to the river had been easy to follow but now he had slowed down, dismounted and was listening. When he heard the voice of Vladimir and Nadia's moans, he climbed a little hill.

From this vantage point, Mikhail could see what was happening. Anna was standing rigid. Vladimir was bending starry-eyed over the diamonds. Behind them there were two men still on their horses; one was holding a knife to Nadia's throat.

Mikhail inched himself into position, leaned up against the tree, and took aim. He hated this part of his work—but these were the enemies of the royal family.

The rifle cracked, and Vladimir fell, the diamonds still clutched in his hand.

Instantly the rider holding Nadia let her drop to the ground, then both rebels spurred their horses into a full gallop—escaping.

Mikhail aimed at one and with deadly accuracy pulled the trigger again. The shot rang out; there was a blood-curdling yell as the man straightened, then fell. Before Mikhail could load again, the other rider was out of sight.

Further down the river, there was another shot. Then a deathly silence.

Anna crawled to Nadia, and pulled her into the shelter of a boulder. Nadia's eyes were rolling back with pain, as she crumpled into an unconscious heap.

Then she crept around the boulder for another look. Who was out there? The shot down the river must be Boris—but who was the sniper? Who else knew about the jewelry? She was afraid to look.

Then she heard a voice behind her. "It's me, Mikhail. Don't worry, Anna. You are finally safe."

Anna slumped against the boulder. Safe! They were safe. She and Nadia were safe.

Mikhail went to gather all the gems from Vladimir's possession and folded them back into the cloth. He also checked the body for any vital signs then covered his face with his jacket.

Picking up the gems, Mikhail went back to Anna and there sitting down on a stump, he opened the cloth. "This isn't all of them," he said. "I know there were a lot more."

Anna hesitated. Her mind wasn't functioning. His voice was muffled. She had seen so much violence—nothing was registering.

He waited patiently. 'Anna? Where's the rest? These must have come from the bigger stash."

The sky was overcast now; it was beginning to sprinkle. She went to the rock, bent over and brushed away the leaves. She picked up the tin box, swept the debris from it, and stood up. "This is it," she said softly. "This is all that we have." She sat down opposite him cradling Nadia who had fallen asleep again.

He took the box, opened it.

"Congratulations, Anna—you have done it. You have completed your mother's wishes and I will give a full report to the royal family. They will probably want to meet you and extend their gratitude personally. I am so proud. We are cousins, you know."

She looked into his eyes. "Cousins?"

That's why he looked so familiar. That's why he looked so much like Aaron. Viktor was his father—the estate—it was all falling into place. "Martha was your mother?"

He nodded.

"Why didn't you tell us when you came?"

"I was on official state business and didn't want to compromise my position. Besides I wanted to have an objective look at this community my parents talked so highly of…."

"Highly of us? She was excommunicated—both banned from the villages…."

"They respected that but still yearned for it—which is why they kept in discreet contact with your mother…."

Anna nodded. "My mother loved them too…very much. But now that you have seen us at our worst…." Her voice trailed.

Mikhail studied this young woman sitting opposite him and realized that he felt nothing but admiration and love for this cousin of his whom he suspected was a lot like her mother. Suddenly he understood his father's yearnings to be near this family. He had great admiration for Anna, Aaron, Neufeld and this newcomer Johann. Except perhaps for Loepky he had a great respect for these people who had proven themselves to be hard working and truthful.

"I've come to admire your family, Anna. I've even come to…" he paused. How should he put it? "I've even come to admire your God. You exude a faith I've rarely seen. I want to know more…. Is it possible for a Russian such as I to be welcomed…" he hesitated.

"Oh yes, Mikhail," Anna wanted to hug him but Nadia was breathing so softly, it would have been cruel to disturb her. "You are already respected and sought after. If the others would know your connection, they would welcome you immediately." She paused, "… as for God. You only have to open up your heart—as I sense you are already doing—and he will flood your being. He will teach you, guide you and reveal all the treasures inside of you."

Then Anna burst into tears and laughter. "Look at us now—if this isn't the perfect illustration of how to find treasure. It hasn't been easy. We've been challenged like no other time in my life, but the rewards, the learnings, the strengthening of the love between us all." She thought of her love for Nadia, for Boris, for Neufeld… they had all grown. Even her relationship with her stepparents was changing—healing. "This is such a perfect example of a search for treasure within us…." She giggled at the thought.

"Oh Mikhail, I can't believe you are my cousin! We will have such a good time getting to know each other now."

"Yes," he said, feeling the power of her love already. He stood up.

"I'm going back to St. Petersburg. I want to take these jewels back and finish my assignment—but I want to come back and revisit you, and I think I want to…."

Before he could finish his sentence, another shot rang out. Mikhail's eyes widened with surprise. His forehead burst into a fountain of blood and he fell in front of her.

She dropped to her knees, desperately trying to hold him, to cling to him, and refuse to let him slip away. They had just met as cousins, but his eyes, which had been brimming with hope and love, now turned empty as he faded away.

Anna turned. It was Loepky standing there in the clearing, a gun in his hands. "You?" she gasped. "What are you doing here?"

"Oh, yes," Loepky said, grinning. "What a pretty scene we have here. Bodies littered all over the place, and jewels, beautiful gems worth so much—right here before me."

His hair, white, was the same; the suit was the same, but the eyes were different. They were now glittering like the jewels. Who was this man? "What interest does the church have in the jewels?" she asked, puzzled.

"Who said anything about the church? These are my ticket to America."

She shook her head. "You just killed someone for these jewels?"

"Criminals," he said.

"You don't know that. You want these for yourself?" She couldn't fathom what she was hearing or seeing.

"Yes, just for me. I'm not even sure I'm taking my wife." He was smiling broadly. "I can start a new life there. This is freedom for me."

"And you condemned me because I read Russian literature, and you yourself scheme to steal, murder and abandon the church?"

He winked at her.

The wink said it all. "You preach damnation, hell fire…."

"And people believe it…." he said still smiling, taking the box of jewels from Mikhail still holding the box.

Slowly she was understanding. Of all of them, he was the worst. The revolutionaries were fighting for a cause—misguided perhaps, but at least they had a cause. Mikhail had some legitimate interest in the gems he was on a mission. But this man, a Mennonite pastor, was operating on greed alone. He was by far the worst.

"No," she said firmly. "Not you. You are not going to have these."

The others couldn't die for nothing—just to allow this man to have the jewels. Her mother, burdened with this secret, would not want it all to turn out like this. There had to be some good that could come out of all of this.

She grabbed the box from him. Then with lightning speed, she grabbed the box from him and turned to run. She heard a shot. A bullet whizzed by her. She picked up her skirt and kept running.

She could not allow these precious jewels to be stolen from her own community. After all the blood shed for them, after all the pain and energy to keep them hidden until the rightful owner asked for them, she could not let them get into the wrong hands.

She heard another shot. But it didn't matter anymore. She had to do what was right. All her life she had been trying to avoid pain, but she couldn't do that anymore. She had discovered that taking the easy way, avoidance, was in the long run more harmful. She would rather die in action than live with the guilt of inaction. She continued to run.

There was another shot, this time from another direction. She heard a yell. She stopped and looked around. It was Loepky, wide-eyed, stumbling towards her, still pointing his gun. There was another shot, and he fell.

She turned it was Boris standing at the bottom of the hill.

"I killed him," he said in a hoarse whisper.

He slumped to his knees. "I killed a Mennonite pastor… This killing is too much for me."

She ran to him and kneeled down beside him, putting her arms around him. "It was the right thing to do," she said, rocking him. "It was the right thing to do."

He clung to her. "I don't think so," he said. "Anna, I think I just killed the minister of your church."

"He wasn't our minister, Boris. We don't know who he was."

"I saw him threatening you—and I reached for the gun and I—shot him."

There were tears running down his face.

She could understand his anguish. He had just wanted to save her life.

She held him close. "He wanted to kill me for the jewels. It was the right thing to do," she reassured him. "It's time to go home."

She paused. "It's time we take Nadia from this cruel mess and go back to your place."

Somehow, they managed to place Nadia on one of the horses—then Boris rounded up the other horses and they rode home in silence.

Once at the estate, with the help of the good doctor and Aaron who seemed able even if he did complain about a headache, they got Nadia into bed and checked on Johann. He was sleeping.

"This estate has become a temporary hospital," the doctor said making his rounds.

Anna sank into the easy chair. All she could think of was Mikhail—her new-found cousin that she had lost as quickly as she had found him. How did this all happen. She glanced over at Boris who seemed of a clear mind again.

"I'm going to go to see Neufeld," Boris said, picking up his hat. "Neufeld will know what to do.

Chapter EIGHTEEN

The house was dark. The horrific images of the day began to finally have their way with her.

Nadia clenched her teeth. She remembered the gun fight at the lagoon, the dead bodies falling to the ground, something about the jewels being found, the painful ride back to the house, the probing doctor, and then the waves and waves of pain that just wouldn't stop.

Her head felt as if it had shattered into a thousand pieces; all sense of time was lost with everything else. She was caught in a wasteland of agony with no beginning, no end. It seemed every nerve in her body was pierced with broken shards of glass. She didn't think she was capable of ever moving again.

There was really only one way to deal with this pain. Nadia let out an ear-splitting, blood-curdling screech.

She was doomed. She had betrayed Anna. It wasn't the cat that killed the swallows—it wasn't Anna's fault. All of this—the dying, the hurting, and the discomfort—all of it was her fault. She continued to scream—a scream that penetrated the entire darkness of the night and then descended into the inner hell of the earth, ending as a weary guttural moan, just as awful as the scream.

"Knocked on the head once too often." That's what her mother had said. The words had been prophetic. The dark inky patches had stretched into lakes, even oceans, and her mind was now one black void. She had been sucked into the bottomless windy blackness and all she wanted was to die.

Anna woke when she heard the first scream—a scream that sent shivers of horror through every nerve in her body. She had never heard such pain before. She knew the scream. She recognized the pain, and she groped her way down the long hallways of Boris' mansion to Nadia's room.

Nadia had curled herself into a tight moaning ball, emitting sounds too dreadful for any ear.

Seeing Anna come into the room, Nadia flung herself back into a stretched cross-like position, and hurled out a string of profanities, words Anna had never heard anyone use before. It was too horrible. She wanted to flee the room, but there was something in the pain that drew her in. This was her pain too.

She tried to soothe Nadia's tortured soul, but there were no words. She tried to embrace the flailing body, but there was no comfort.

Finally, Anna stood back, watching the writhing agony, wondering, remembering, and praying to know the source. She tried to recall the beginning of this change in Nadia, the cause of this pain.

She remembered. The change in Nadia had begun after the first beating by the revolutionaries. Anna had been too preoccupied to pursue the matter, but it was as if a dark cloud had rolled in between them. A cloud of fear, anger—and there was something else. Anna struggled to remember what it was; Nadia's peace of mind depended on it. Slowly she remembered more. Nadia, showing up, following her back to the villages, and then back to Boris' house, her eyes becoming darker with increasing pain, dark with fear, dark with…? Why did Nadia follow her? None of this made sense. Then there was the scene at the lagoon with Nadia coming to her, calling to her with the three men—luring her into their trap, betraying her. And then Anna knew.

Anna knelt on the bed, and took hold of Nadia's shoulders. "Nadia, listen to me. Nadia listen to me!"

When the girl did not respond, she gently cupped Nadia's face in her hands. The eyes were vacant. Anna began to sing a simple song, the only song that came to her mind. *Gott ist die liebe.*

Slowly Nadia's eyes began to focus, but the pain in them was unbelievable. There was silence.

Anna heard the cock crow outside the window. The day was breaking, and she knew how to do it. It had been done before.

"Nadia, do you love me?"

There were instant tears; the eyes opened but there were no words, only a new visible anguish of the soul in the dark eyes. Anna could almost see the receding of the mind into the dark memories, too dark.

"Nadia," Anna paused. The girl was paying attention, watching her, slightly bewildered. Anna needed to take advantage of every moment. "Do you really—really—love me?" Anna asked again. The tears were back in a burst of convulsive sobs, ending with one long scream from the depths of darkness and hell.

The girl choked on a wrenching sob. Nodding her head, she started to moan.

Anna paused. She knew it wasn't enough. She took a deep breath.

Anna held her breath. She had to pull Nadia out of herself; she had to hang on to this last thread of consciousness. Anna repeated the question slowly, prayerfully, but forcefully. "Nadia, do you love me as a *schwester*?"

Nadia began to shake violently. Waves and waves of pain, guilt and remorse flooded over her body. Then the expression of pain went inward. This was the dangerous moment. Would Nadia ever have the courage to surface again? Anna hung onto Nadia, rocking her, murmuring words of encouragement until Nadia's pain finally dissolved into a whimper.

"Then, Nadia, I need you to forgive yourself."

With a gasp, Nadia threw her arms around Anna and held onto her tightly as if she would never let go again—ever. The sobs were those of a child. The darkness was receding.

Anna stroked her hair. "I love you, Nadia," she whispered. "We've all done things these last few days that we regret. I feel I have failed my mother. I feel I have failed my cousin, Mikhail. I feel I have failed Boris. I've failed you, and the entire community. But a long time ago my mother said, 'We strive too much to live by right and wrong—when really we should strive to apply and exercise lavish mercy.' Lavish mercy, Nadia. Lavish—wonderful—lavish mercy is what we all need. I will give it to you."

And then they both cried for a long time in each other's arms.

A shadow hovering near the bedroom door, slowly moved away from the door, down the hall, to his bedroom. Johann sat down on the edge of his bed.

He had heard the screaming, and had gone to check, ignoring his painful shoulder. He had seen Anna go into Nadia's room, and had hovered at the door, waiting to see if she would need help. This was the second time he had found himself eavesdropping on an important moment in her life. Each time her beauty had mesmerized him.

Tonight, in her white nightgown, sitting with Nadia, candle by the bedside, she seemed almost surreal, her sensual beauty enchanting. It was just another of the many pictures that would haunt him: Anna sitting in the huge chair by the fire, riding astride the horse—her skirt up around her thighs, standing so regally in the church, and baking zwieback in that silk dress.

But it wasn't only her beauty which had captivated him, it was the way she had handled Nadia. Anna hadn't been afraid of the screams; she had gone to Nadia in absolute love. And then she had used the model of Jesus' conversation with Peter to help Nadia—which was exactly what Nadia had needed to face the demons of guilt. Anna had essentially healed Nadia's guilt and shame. How had Anna known?

Nadia, do you really, really love me? The words would be forever imprinted in his memory—the daring, the love, and the wisdom.

Johann swallowed hard—feeling the emotion of it all. Anna had no idea that her words had reached beyond the room to his own demons. Lavish mercy, she had said. It wasn't only about being right, doing right; it was about lavish mercy. He would forever understand the word *lavish* in a different way. It was an overabundance of grace to cover everything that had gone wrong.

Tonight, seeing Anna looking after Nadia, saying those words, redeeming the soul of a Russian servant, he knew never again could he condemn her for anything. In hindsight, all that about Russian literature seemed so petty in the face of the love that he had just witnessed. Her wisdom was God's wisdom.

Chapter NINETEEN

A week later, Neufeld made his way to Boris' estate which had truly become a makeshift hospital for Aaron, Johann and Nadia who were still too weak to travel. Some of the women in the community had dropped in periodically to help Anna look after them.

He knew what his role was here. At the news of Loepky's death, by default, he was now the lead pastor and commissioned to bring peace and harmony back to their community.

Now they were waiting for him in the living room.

There was Nadia, lying on the sofa, wincing in pain every time she moved. There was Johann sitting in an easy chair, still tender, but already looking like his former self. Then Anna, in the other easy chair sat opposite him, with a new look of determination in her eyes, but unusually pale and listless. Aaron looked extremely uncomfortable, stiff and confused.

Boris was the only one who seemed to have survived it all in good spirits. His eyes were clear and lucid.

From what Neufeld understood, it had taken a great deal of effort to find and bring back the bodies of the three rebels, housing them in the tack room before shipping them to Nyevinnomissk where they were buried unceremoniously in a Catholic cemetery.

Then there had been the funeral for Loepky, which had been well attended but devoid of emotion. Loepky's wife was stunned at the news of her husband's death but even more shamed when she realized what he had been scheming to do. She had withdrawn into her own voluntary shunning, it seemed.

And then there had been Mikhail Kamensky. At Anna's suggestion they had buried him as one of their own organizing an elaborate funeral which had been well attended by the most interesting of crowds including the bar tender Slepkov and his tavern clientele to other Okhrana agents, church members and even some of the Russian peasant farmers. The story of his last conversation with Anna had been truly inspiring.

Neufeld cleared his throat. "There is not going to be a formal investigation," he began. They looked visibly relieved. "Except for the death of Reverend Loepky, it seems apparent as to what happened. The Russian police are leaving the investigation of the death of Loepky to the church."

There was a tension in the room. Nadia glanced at Boris....

"We have been investigating it," he too glanced at Boris – who was smiling and apparently oblivious to any sense of guilt.

"Apparently the majority in the church have for some time realized that Reverend Loepky was becoming mean-spirited and distracted. However, that he embezzled money from the church has taken everyone by surprise. Many feel betrayed and angry. We, as a community, will need to take great care in meting out justice. Our history is full of violence against us; we know how to deal with that. We are not as skilled in dealing with criminal behavior in our own community. We usually banish those we can't deal with. Loepky is dead. Yet his presence lingers. We all need to come to terms with what he did and what that means to our church."

He looked down. The tin box filled with the jewels was sitting right in front of him on the coffee table, an array of gems the likes of which he had never seen before. He didn't need to be told the value or the importance of them.

He cleared his throat again and continued. "There was a letter in Mikhail's possessions as to the nature of this assignment with instructions about what he was to do after he found the jewels. It reads that he was to handsomely reward all those who looked after the jewels, and were involved in the recovery of them. The rest is to be sent back to the owner, Ella, who will be using the money from the sale of the jewels to build a convent. She had dedicated her life to helping the poor.

"Anna, I will return the two brooches that were your mother's. And you are also to have the diamond necklace." He then allowed the rest to choose the piece of jewelry they preferred.

There was no reaction to the wealth they had now attained. Nothing. No response. The jewelry had been tarnished.

Neufeld knew this wouldn't be easy. It never was. Violence always left a stain. And while with some valiant effort they might be able to get the stain out, the effort would always leave its own telltale residue. But they were resilient; they had each other. The Mennonite church, a church of peace, had endured much violence and persecution. The church understood suffering. They would be looked after. But right now, he needed to give them comfort.

He continued. "I don't know what happened by the river but to feel the threat of death, and to see others die, is never easy. As a Mennonite community we abhor violence. We seek peace. But violence is part of our nature, and part of the world in which we live. There is forgiveness in all of this."

"Anna and Aaron, your mother Elizabeth used to tell us that we as a community lived too closely to judgment and that we needed to remember that God was really all about mercy. I think that belief is what made her a very joyful, accepting and wonderful person. I think above all she would be proud of each one of you."

At this both Anna and Aaron were visibly moved. Silent tears were coursing down their cheeks.

"At times like this, I usually read the 23rd Psalm.

Even though I walk through a valley dark as death
I fear no evil, for you are with me,
Thy staff and thy crook are my comfort.
Thou spreadest a table for me in the sight of my enemies;
Thou hast richly bathed my head with oil,
And my cup runs over.

Goodness and love unfailing, these will follow me
All the days of my life,
And I shall dwell in the house of the Lord
My whole life long."

Neufeld took off his glasses. There was still a heaviness that hung over the group.

Then, Neufeld bowed his head saying a healing prayer for each one of them.

When he looked up. He noticed Boris—grinning.

Boris then stood up, went into the kitchen and in seconds came back with a tray of drinks for everyone—his famous juice. Boris presented the tray to Neufeld first. Neufeld smiled, took a glass, and they all did likewise. He held up his glass. "To better times."

It was a signal to all that this was going to be a new era. Under Neufeld the village would begin to experience a new peace and order—and even more than that, a new freedom and acceptance.

It was an impromptu party like no other.... The buggies started coming onto the yard mid-afternoon and soon Boris' estate house and yard was full of guests mingling as they automatically began to set up the tables and chairs for what appeared to be an early supper for the entire community.

No doubt, the star feature for the event was the Fabergé jewels. And apparently, everyone was coming—except for Widow Wieler who claimed a headache—but her children, Jakob, Lisa and Marie came intrigued with not only the jewelry but with the new status of prestige they had acquired by just having a few pieces of the Fabergé jewels now attached to their name.

At some point, all the guests made their way into the living room, eager to see the jewels displayed on the center coffee table. They took their time, examining the precious gems, admiring their beauty, and some even ogling at their brilliance. A few guests went as far as touching the jewels, and a handful even dared to try on the necklaces, all while Boris stood guard, keeping a watchful eye on the valuable display.

No one could deny the power of the jewels or their story of intrigue.

It was all becoming too much for Anna and she found herself sitting on the top of the staircase watching the commotion below, wanting to be part of the party and yet wanting to remain near Nadia who had gone back to her bed.

She could see Johann, who had been mingling with the guests comfortably, was now sitting off to the side with Beth. Anna felt a pang. She had come to appreciate him—so much—remembering the chase through the night, their conversations, the gunshot, the heroism, the stolen kiss.... She lingered at the memory of that kiss. Then shook her head. It was obvious to her and everyone else in that room that he now belonged to Beth. And they looked good together—sitting in the corner deep in conversation. They were probably committing themselves to each other.... Anna looked away. She couldn't bear the sight of it.

But just as she was about to get up, she noticed Neufeld climbing the stairs to join her.

He sat down beside her. "Fascinating," he said. "The jewelry has power."

Anna nodded. "I knew my mother was wonderful but I didn't realize the extent of her influence."

"Yes," agreed Neufeld. "She was a very gracious woman known for her kindness, her insight, and her sensitivity. She would be proud of this all."

"I am grieving Mikhail. I was just getting to know him. I think he would have been a wonderful addition our community. He had so much potential," she whispered.

"And I am grieving Loepky and what he has done to this community. I'm glad it came out. It was a needed revelation for all of us." Neufeld cleared his throat. "Which brings me to something else that we need to talk about. Loepky was the one who was pushing for your excommunication—as well as your stepfather and your stepmother. This changes everything. I think we now have a new perspective of worldliness. I think we realize that the evil is not out there in Boris' library. But that it can reside in us and even in our church."

Neufeld sighed. "I think we're entering into a time of grace now. You and your mother are showing us the way. We must always fight our instinctive desire to harshly judge and marginalize those within our own community. These jewels have revealed ourselves to ourselves and for that I'm grateful. And I'm sorry for all that you have had to go through. I do know that you are loved by the community and you have gained respect in all of our hearts."

Anna could feel the tears well up in her eyes. "Thank you. Those words mean a lot to me. I think my mother has been a great example to me and I know now that I just need to follow in her footsteps…." Anna paused. "I think I'm going to have to make some changes in my own life. I can't go back to live with my stepfather and stepmother. Boris has hinted that Nadia and I can stay here and help with his house…. He does need help. We will include Aaron as well if he wants to come. What is your counsel?"

"Excellent," Neufeld said with a smile. "I think it is time to go out on your own with Aaron to find a place that will welcome you. I see God's guidance in all of this."

Anna heard a soft whimper coming from Nadia's room. "I think Nadia needs me…."

Neufeld stood up as well. "Feel blessed my child."

Chapter TWENTY

And then the party was over and they were gone. Just as quickly as they had appeared in their buggies on foot and on their horses, they left—leaving the yard spotless. Perhaps even better than before. This was the community that she was proud of. They could work together like no other and accomplish things like no other.

She stepped outside onto the veranda. The moon had come out and it was warm outside—the air felt like velvet.

Suddenly she wanted to be with her mother again to tell her of everything that had happened and to thank her. She stepped inside to tell Boris that she was going for a walk.

He smiled. "It is safe—but do take Canon with you."

With Canon at her side, Anna crossed the yard and started down the trail to the hiding place.

She could feel her mother. She followed the trail, over the hills, along the river till finally she reached the lagoon and sat down leaning against a tree.

There she found the peace she was looking for. She talked to her mother, talked to her God, sang a few songs—then closed her eyes envisioning her mother in heaven coming down to embrace her.

She was just about to go back when Canon sensed something—stood up—growling a warning.

There was movement—someone was coming down the trail. "Canon—it's me." It was Johann's voice.

Canon went to greet him.

"Can I join you?" Johann hesitated emerging out of the shadows.

"Yes of course." She patted the spot beside her. "I was just about to go back but come sit with me. It is lovely out here. Quiet and beautiful."

He sat down beside her—and they just sat there…for a long moment—awkwardly.

Then he cleared his throat. "I did want to talk to you about something." Johann began, his voice low. "I saw Neufeld speaking with you on the stairs and I realize that he probably was talking about the Russian literature. I hope he was telling you that in the light of this week's events, it is now a non-issue in the church. They have removed the motion."

"Yes, he did." Anna answered. "He told me that things have changed. That Loepky's actions have made a difference. Everyone has realized again that books are not the evil that has scarred our church, greed is." She paused. "But I am learning too. I think that I will still read Russian literature but I will be more careful. I had a good mentor in my mother who read only the good books, but not everyone does. Children are highly influenced and we need to take care of what we expose them to. I know that now. But it was good to hear that it is now a non-issue for the church and that I am now accepted for who I am."

Johann nodded. "I think this is a new beginning for the church—for all of us—in a lot of ways."

Anna agreed. "Best of all my mother is being recognized for who she was. I think Neufeld and I both agreed that the jewels have made a difference in the way we see things now."

Johann ran a hand through his hair. "I know I feel differently about a lot of things. I came here looking for a place to settle. I had heard so many good things about the Kuban villages so I came to check it out. I suppose I came at a very critical moment and I have learned a lot—not only about the villages but about jewels, guns, Okhrana agents and what it feels like getting shot in the shoulder," he chuckled.

Anna laughed, "And I was learning how to ride a horse again—how to run through puddles of mud…," she paused. "I never did learn how to stop Boris from shooting at everyone."

They both laughed. It was good to laugh.

"And I want to learn more," Johann continued. "There are still so many pieces missing…." He paused and stood up. “For example, I don’t even know what happened at the shootout. Is this where it all happened?”

“Actually, we are close to where the jewels were hidden.” Anna stood up. “I can show you.”

“Good—want to know it all,” he stood up.

She led the way to the cliff and then where the rocks turned into steps.

“First of all, I was standing here when Vladimir came with his buddies. Mikhail shot from that hill and then Mikhail was standing about there—near that tree….” She paused. It was still hard to think back to that moment. “… and Boris shot Loepky from there.”

“What a nightmare!”

“And the jewelry was here.” She said leading the way.

She could feel his nearness as they climbed up the steps to the crevice. It was large enough for one person, two if they squeezed. He was very, very close.

She reached up; her fingers finding the narrow ledge.

“It was here,” she said taking his hand and guiding it to find the ledge where the tin case had been hidden—now empty and dark.

His hand explored the empty shelf with hers and then stopped. They were squeezed tightly together and he wasn’t moving. She was caught pressed against his body. Initially, she wanted to push her way out but slowly that urge melted away as his hand lifted her face up to meet his eyes. In the moonlit darkness they gazed at each other, allowing their heart to speak without words.

All he could think of was Anna—Beth paled in comparison. The picture of Anna sitting in that wingback chair surrounded by books, riding the horse, baking the buns, sitting by the church window, in the barn finding the Bible—the scene of her and Nadia and the way she had cared for him when he had been shot. He ran his fingers through her dark auburn hair—then his lips found hers.

Anna was immediately lost in the sensual softness of his lips pressed against hers, their moistness impossible to resist as their lips parted ever so gently. His other hand circled her waist pulling her even closer until they became one as his lips moved with deliberate slowness from her lips to her cheeks and down to her neck, igniting a string of fires that set her soul ablaze. In response, she raised her arms to embrace him, her fingers tracing the nape of his neck, cherishing the touch of his beautiful black hair.

She had never felt so safe, so loved, so sensually beautiful—never wanting to let go. Never wanting this enchanting intimacy to end.

Then slowly, tenderly he pulled back—his finger touching her lips.

"We need to…stop." He stepped back, took her hand and led her back to the lagoon, then leaned her against the tree and kissed her again.

"I don't want to stop," he said. "You are driving me insane."

She understood—to stay might mean that the insanity of passion might take over with vehemence. "Let's go back to the house," she said softly.

"Yes," he said but did not let go of her hand the entire way back to the mansion. It was wonderful just to walk hand in hand in the dark without a word. She wished it would never end.

Canon followed them at a distance, chasing imaginary night life then, seemingly caught up in the moment, he danced between them.

At the edge of the yard, Johann stopped.

The sight of the mansion left her feeling conflicted—relieved to be home but sad that this moment with Johann was being broken. All she could think of was how wonderful it had been to be together searching the ledge where her mother had hidden the jewelry. She remembered her mother's words—"To find love is more precious than any gold." At that moment, Johann had felt more precious than the Fabergé. Was this passion or was this love? She searched her heart, it was love, she decided. It would remain unrequited love; she knew he belonged to Beth. Beth was everything he would want, rich, blonde and beautiful.

Johann turned and touched her cheek. "These kisses need to be honored."

What did that mean? Anna wondered.

"And there is only one way to honor them."

Honor? How does one honor stolen kisses—passionate sinful kisses? She was baffled. She wanted to relish the memory of them—that would be enough. The memory could and would last a lifetime. They didn't need to be honored—just forgiven—eventually.

"Anna, I love you," he said softly.

She gasped.

"Do you love me?' he whispered.

It was as if the heavens opened. "Oh yes…," she breathed, "but what about Beth…?"

He paused…. "She'll understand—there is someone else for her. I've already kind of hinted that I wasn't ready…."

"You knew before this moment?"

"Not with the clarity of this moment. It is these kisses that convince me," he chuckled, kissing her again.

"No—it's not just the kisses. I've been giving it some thought. If we marry…. We could live here—all of us together. The house is big enough for your Nadia and Aaron—and my mother and sister…."

What was he talking about?

He hesitated, groping for words. "My dream of buying this house fits very well with yours…. That is, if you…would like to marry me?" He paused…. He went down on his knees and then in a very formal voice asked softly. "Anna, will you marry…"

He didn't need to finish.

"Oh yes," she breathed, her eyes wide and brimming with tears.

She reached down to touch his cheeks…. "Yes, yes, yes. I will marry you!"

"This is the most wonderful moment of my life," he said getting up.

Then his lips lowered to find hers again—and they were lost in the moment.

They kissed again and again—and this time the kisses were complete in and of themselves. Pure, promising a new love—a forever freedom.

Canon sensed it all and entered into the gleeful moment with them—barking happily with joy.

The front door opened.

The End

Glossary OF TERMS

Map

Kuban villages - founded in 1863

Lower village - Alexandrodar—previously known as Alexanderfeld (1890)

Upper village - Vyikoknyazheskoye—previously known as Wohldemfurerst (1890)

Molotschna & Chortitza - two settlements in the Ukraine—mother colonies

Caucasian Railway - completed in 1875

Mount Elbrus -18,480 feet, highest mountain the Caucasus Mountain Range

Family

Abram Franz - Oberschulz (Mayor) of the two Kuban villages

Elizabeth - first wife of Abram Franz

Widow Wieler - (Gertrude) second wife of Abram Franz

Anna Franz - stepdaughter of Mayor and Widow Wieler

Aaron Franz - stepson of Mayor and Widow Wieler

Jakob - son of Widow Wieler

Maria - daughter of Widow Wieler

Lisa - daughter of Widow Wieler

Church Leaders

Cornelius Neufeld - minister

George Loepky - lead pastor

Isaac Thiessen - elder and deacon

Joseph Schellenberg - trustee and church treasurer

Johann Baerg - council member

David Baerg - itinerant minister

Claus Rempel - estate owner (daughters Beth & Rina)

Mark Froese - village doctor

Russians

Okhrana - political police force

Mikhail Kamensky - Okhrana agent

Viktor Kamensky - assistant to Governor Grand Duke

Martha Kamensky - Viktor's wife (Elizabeth's sister)

Vladimir Kuusinen - socialist

Lev Slepkov - tavern owner

Boris Balakirev - General

Vera Balakirev - Boris' wife

Nadia - Boris' niece

Canon - Boris' dog

Terms

Aeltester - bishop

blin - shit

bliatz - bitch

bubliki - bagel-like dumplings, poached and baked, often sold at Russian markets

brooch - Fabergé pin

crokinole - traditional dexterity game—a lot like table curling

durak - fool

faspa - a lunch often served Sunday late afternoon

Gott ist die liebe. - God is love.

kon 'pedal'nii - idiot

loh - loser

oberschulz - colony administrator

perishke - small pocket pastry with meat or fruit filling

prips - barley-based drink often substituted for coffee

plautz - rich baking powder crust covered with fruit and crumble topping

reesche - tweebach toasted zwieback which could last for months, often dunked in coffee

schwester - sister

schulz - mayor

verst - Russian measure of distance equal to just over a kilometer (.66 miles)

zwieback - a double bun

About the Author

As a writer, Wilma Derksen brings a unique blend of personal experiences, professional expertise in trauma and resilience, and a hidden love for romance to her storytelling. Her passion for crafting love stories resonates in her work, captivating readers with intriguing historical settings and imperfect characters finding their perfect matches.

Wilma currently resides in Winnipeg, Canada.

WilmaDerksen.com

Manufactured by Amazon.ca
Bolton, ON

35726475R00138